Birthday Cake and I Scream

Look for these SpineChillers™ Mysteries

Birthday Cake and I Scream

Fred E. Katz

Thomas Nelson, Inc.

Nashville

Published in Nashville, Tennessee, by Tommy Nelson™, a division of Thomas Nelson, Inc. SpineChillers™ Mysteries is a trademark of Thomas Nelson, Inc.

Scripture quoted from the *International Children's Bible, New Century Version,* copyright © 1986, 1988 by Word Publishing. Used by permission.

Storyline: Tim Ayers

ISBN 0–8499–4062–1

Printed in the United States of America

97 98 99 00 01 02   QKP   9 8 7 6 5 4 3 2 1

In a few days I was going to be twelve years old. You'd think that a guy's twelfth birthday should be special. I expected mine to be, but the best places to hold a party weren't cooperating.

I wanted to take a huge group of friends to play paintball. But when my mom called Pete's Paintball, it already had a party booked for Friday night.

Mom and I called all over town after that, looking for a fun place to celebrate my birthday. But we kept hearing over and over, "Sorry, but we're booked that night."

I had completely run out of ideas and hated the thought of having the party at home. My folks and I live in a small house with a little yard. It's not big enough for the number of friends I wanted to include. I'd have to uninvite a bunch of kids. I thought that would be the worst thing in the world. That is until Mom gave me the "good news."

When I came home from school, I tossed my

backpack on the floor by the door and headed to the kitchen. After a long day at school and soccer practice, I needed to refuel with chocolate chip cookies and a big glass of milk.

As I poured myself a tall glass of cow juice, Mom came home from work. She didn't even put her briefcase down before she excitedly said, "Kiddo (she always calls me Kiddo, but you can call me Mac—MacKenzie Richard Griffin's the name), I have good news for the birthday boy."

"You decided to get me a four-wheeler?" I jokingly asked.

"Even better—I found a place for your party."

My face lit up, and my feet felt like dancing. "Where?"

"Spookie the Clown's Halls of Pizza," she announced with a beaming smile.

My face went gray, and my dancing feet became lead. "Mom, we can't go there!" I said.

She knit her brows in puzzlement and asked, "Why?"

"It's for little kids," I protested. "I'll be the laughingstock of the century."

"Don't worry. You and your friends will have the entire Halls of Pizza to yourselves." Mom smiled. "And Spookie the Clown told me they have a room filled with the latest video games. They even have your favorite, Guardians."

"Guardians? They've got Guardians? Hardly anyone has that one."

Mom made a good argument. If we had the place to ourselves, we wouldn't be bothered by little kids. And the games didn't hurt. But I wasn't convinced. "What about the important stuff like—"

"Like good food?" Mom interrupted. "You'll have all the pizza you can eat. Speaking of which, if we want to eat tonight, I better get moving." Mom headed to her bedroom to change out of her work clothes.

I sat at the kitchen table thinking while I polished off my glass of milk and three cookies. Mom had convinced *me* that Spookie's place could be fun. Could I convince my friends?

I felt uneasy, so I decided I'd wait until lunchtime the next day to tell anyone. Lots of people had planned to come to my party on Friday night. Would they change their minds when I told them to meet me at a place for little kids?

My morning classes went fast. As much as I liked lunchtime, I hadn't looked forward to this one. I was lost in thought as I entered the cafeteria. I heard Frankie call out, "Hey, over here."

I snapped my head up and noticed that I had almost walked right past our table. I gave her and my best friend, Barry, an embarrassed smile.

"Earth to MacKenzie, earth to MacKenzie," Barry

said, imitating the scratchy sound of an old science fiction movie. "Please land at your earliest convenience."

I absently started to sit down and nearly plopped down on Lisa. She had slipped into the seat as I was snapping out of my what-do-I-tell-my-friends trance. "Sorry, Lisa. I didn't see you come up behind me."

Lisa smiled at me as I settled into the chair next to hers. I was with my three closest friends, and I dreaded what I had to say.

Barry Lennon had seen most of my twelve years with me. He lived right behind me. We'd played together, gone to the same schools, and attended the same Bible class at church for as long as I could remember.

Frankie and Lisa were cousins. They went to our church too. Lisa spent a lot of time at Frankie's house, which was only a few blocks from mine. Barry and I often walked down to join them. And, since they shared the last name Grey, the girls and I had sat next to each other in all of our elementary school classes. Our teachers had this thing about seating us alphabetically.

Frankie and Lisa were the most fun girls I knew. The four of us played on the same ball teams and attended the same youth group. I guess a person could say that we were inseparable. I hated to tell them my news about Spookie's.

"I have some bad news," I began as a warning.

4

That immediately got everyone's attention. I was ready to drop the news about Spookie's.

Then Davis Wong scooted into the seat at the end of the table and asked, "So, when do I get my paintball gun, and who wants to get hit first?"

Davis was a recent addition to our group. He had just started at the school this year; his dad was our new vice principal. We had met him during the summer at a youth group meeting. He was a pretty cool kid, and he had a crazy sense of humor.

I didn't know what to do. Without stopping to think, I blurted out, "The paintball place is booked."

"What?" Frankie cried out.

"No paintball?" Davis's mouth drooped into a gigantic frown.

"Are you kidding?" Barry asked.

"No, I'm not kidding. I guess this was a popular weekend for parties. We tried everywhere. Everybody had something going on this Friday night," I reported sorrowfully.

"So, what are you going to do?" Frankie asked with genuine concern.

"We booked Spookie the Clown's Halls of Pizza," I answered.

Frankie asked, "Isn't that the new place in that old building on Tremble Avenue?"

"That's the one," I responded.

Lisa gasped and got a terribly serious look on her

face. Then she sat up straight and said firmly, "No, not Spookie's. Anyplace but Spookie the Clown's Halls of Pizza."

"I figured some people wouldn't want to go because it's a place for little kids," I said. I slumped lower and lower in my chair.

Lisa shot back, "No, that's not it at all. It has nothing to do with little kids. Spookie the Clown's Halls of Pizza is haunted!"

"Come on, Lisa, you don't really believe those silly stories, do you?" Frankie asked.

"I've heard that some pretty strange things have gone on in that old building," her cousin said defensively.

"What happens, do ghosts jump out of pizzas to scare kids?" Davis quipped.

"Don't joke, Davis. There's something very unusual about that building. Nothing stays in business there very long," Barry said.

"Remember last year? Uncle Andy's House of Sandwiches only lasted about four months. When we were little kids, it was the Chunks of Cheese Pizza Parlor. I can't remember all the names that came in between."

Davis looked puzzled. He asked, "Why do you think so many places go out of business there?"

"It's simple," Lisa stated sharply. "The building is haunted, and the ghosts scare away customers."

In all my planning for my birthday party, I hadn't stopped to consider that Spookie's was located in the old Tremble Avenue building.

When my friends and I were a lot younger, the older kids used to tell us stories about that place. They scared us with their talk about ghosts. But that was years ago. We were the older kids now.

Surely Lisa and Barry didn't still believe those crazy stories. Besides, we'd given our lives to Christ. Believing in Jesus and ghosts at the same time just didn't fit.

"Do you think the ghosts are still there? Do you think they'll make a special appearance at Mac's party?" Barry asked us.

The bell rang, interrupting our conversation. We scattered to head to our next classes. As I walked down the hallway, I thought about the ghost stories the older kids used to tell us. There were nights when I had to keep a light on in my room because I was so scared. I felt a shiver run up my spine.

Get a grip on reality, Mac, I told myself. *You've given your life to the Lord, and you're too old to be spooked by silly ghost stories.*

The rest of the school day seemed pretty routine. Even soccer practice just sort of slipped by. We covered the same drills over and over. I guess the coach was looking for perfection, but today my heart just wasn't in the game. I was glad to get out of there.

After practice, I hurried to meet Frankie and Lisa at the town library. We had some research to do for a history report. I had chosen them as study partners because they were the two smartest students in the class.

When I got to the library, they had already started on the report.

"Sorry. Practice went long," I said after I greeted them. "How's the report coming?"

"Not too bad. We've found a lot of information on the Civil War. Our biggest problem is narrowing things down to a single topic," Lisa said.

"Maybe I can help," I offered.

"We were hoping you might contribute something to this team," Frankie said with a grin. "You could start by digging through these books."

Before I sat down, I said, "I saw another book last week that had some unusual Civil War stories in it. It's up on the third floor. It'll only take me a second to grab it."

I remembered that the book had lots of personal stories in it. Some quotes from people who had fought in the war could make our report outstanding.

Most people avoided the third floor with its stacks of musty-smelling books. But I liked to prowl and see what new worlds I could discover on the shelves upstairs. I remembered the book was somewhere in the back left corner of the building.

The third floor seemed unusually dim today. After all our talk at lunch about ghosts, the darkness spooked me a little. I walked very slowly between the shelves, listening carefully for sounds that didn't belong in a library.

Finding the book wasn't going to be as easy as I thought. It wasn't where I remembered. I kneeled, trying to focus on the book spines in the dim light.

Suddenly, a large shadow cut off my light. I immediately felt alarmed. What made it? I looked up, but the shadow, and whatever made it, was gone.

I told myself I was being silly. It was probably just someone looking for a book like I was. I went back to my search.

I spotted the book and reached for it with relief.

Then something blocked the light again. This time, when I looked up, I saw a dark form. It did not look like a person. It looked like it had wings.

Gripping my book, I stood up and backed against the wall. The thing moved between the rows of bookshelves—toward me. Its shadow shivered as it approached. Had it seen me?

I scanned the shelves. I wondered if I could climb them and get away. If I tossed books at the approaching menace, would it run?

The form took two more steps and stopped. I placed my foot on one of the shelves to start climbing. But the shelf bowed with my weight. It would never support me.

So I grabbed the heaviest books I could find and waited. If the ghoul came any closer, I was going to clobber it. I heard it taking slow, deep breaths. I wondered if it could hear that my heart had begun to beat like a wild conga drum.

The shadowy figure lunged toward me.

I tensed and aimed one of the heavy books at the shape. Before I could throw it, black cloth fluttered down toward me. In a panic, I fought my way free. In the next second, I realized what had happened.

"That was just a little birthday scare for you," Frankie said through her snorts of laughter.

The girls had threaded long rulers through the arms of Lisa's black raincoat. That's why it looked like it had wings. They had used the creepy shape to scare me.

"Hey, that wasn't funny at all. A guy can get really tense backed into a dark corner like that. If I had hit you with one of these big books, I could have really hurt you," I chastised them both.

Lisa reached out and took one of the books from my hands. She looked at the cover, and her eyes grew wide. "Very appropriate, MacKenzie. Did you choose this book on purpose?"

"No, I just grabbed the fat ones. What is it?" I asked.

Frankie took the book from Lisa. She turned the spine my way. I read the title: *Middletown's Ghosts and Ghouls: And Their Favorite Haunts.*

Frankie handed it back to me. "Are you sure you didn't purposely choose that one?"

"No. I just grabbed it because it was thick. I couldn't even see the spines of the books. Remember, you cut off all my light," I replied.

"Then this whole thing is scaring me. Is there anything in there about the building on Tremble Avenue?" Lisa asked.

I opened the book to the contents page. I scanned the chapter titles and stopped when I reached chapter 13: "The Haunting on Tremble Avenue." I couldn't believe what I had just read. Maybe if I closed my eyes, the words would change. I squeezed them tight and opened them again.

I felt my mouth go dry. I managed to mumble, "You're not going to believe this." Lisa looked at me curiously as I handed her the book.

"Look at chapter thirteen." My voice was barely a squeak.

Lisa gasped.

"What?" Frankie asked, concern registering in her voice.

Lisa didn't answer. She flipped through the pages of the book. When she stopped, she began to read.

"The legend surrounding the building at 1313

Tremble Avenue can be traced back to the turn of the century. At that time Bertrand Bailey Cooley died mysteriously in the room he rented in the building's basement."

Lisa glanced up at me, then turned her eyes back to the book. She licked her lips and continued reading.

"Rumor has it that Cooley had stashed a fortune somewhere inside the building. The means by which Cooley gained such a fortune are uncertain, considering his employment."

Frankie and I stared at Lisa as she turned the page.

"Cooley worked in the building's first-floor restaurant during the winter season. The rest of the year he was employed as a clown in a traveling carnival."

Lisa abruptly stopped reading and looked wide-eyed at Frankie and me. "A clown!" Her voice sounded higher than normal, though she kept it quiet because we were in the library. "And now a clown is running the restaurant! Don't you think that's more than a coincidence?"

"You can't be serious," Frankie said. "The guy you're reading about died almost a hundred years ago. No. It's just a coincidence, Lisa. Keep reading."

I kept my mouth shut. I knew Frankie was right. A clown who had died almost a hundred years ago couldn't be linked to a clown who was alive and running a business today. But still, the thought was unsettling.

"Six months after Cooley's death, another man, Oscar R. Newcombe, also died mysteriously in the Tremble Avenue building," Lisa continued. "Newcombe, the manager of the carnival for which Cooley had worked, was allegedly in search of Cooley's hidden fortune. Newcombe claimed Cooley had stolen the money from the carnival.

"No facts were ever substantiated in the incidents, and no fortune has ever been found. Yet legend has it that the ghosts of Cooley and Newcombe roam the building, frightening anyone who threatens to find the hidden fortune."

I gulped. The fears I'd had as a little kid listening to the ghost stories about the Tremble Avenue building came rushing back. Fortunately, Frankie still had the voice of reason.

"Eerie legend," she said. "But that's all it is. A legend. There's no such thing as ghosts."

"Don't be so sure," Lisa answered. "The next section of the chapter is called, 'Reports of Apparitions and Unexplainable Phenomena.'"

"Hey, we better get to work on our report," I said. I didn't want to hear any more about ghosts, but I didn't want to tell Frankie and Lisa that I was getting spooked.

"Why don't you take this home with you?" Lisa said, handing me the book. "You can read the rest of the chapter later."

I carried the creepy book and the one on the Civil War back to the main floor. We managed to get some work done, though I had trouble staying focused. I wanted to get home. The sun was already going down, and in my current state of mind, I didn't want to walk home in the dark.

The girls were heading to Frankie's, a few blocks from my home. We walked the several blocks from the library together talking about school, ghosts, the youth group, ghosts, other friends, and ghosts.

I was still concerned that some of my friends wouldn't come to my party. After all, Spookie's was for little kids. I wanted to make sure Frankie and Lisa would be there.

"Are you two still coming to my party Friday night?" I looked down at the sidewalk. "I mean, even though we can't have it at Pete's Paintball?"

"Of course we'll be there," Frankie said. "You're our friend, Mac."

I looked up at Frankie. She was smiling.

"It will be a private party," I said in an attempt to play up the positive side. "Mom rented the entire place for the night."

"Aren't you two scared of that building after what we read in that book?" Lisa asked.

"I don't see how a pizza place for little kids could be haunted. Isn't there some kind of law against that?" Frankie questioned.

I joked, "It's in the *Ghosts and Ghouls Rule Book*."

We had come to Frankie's house. I watched until the girls were safely inside. Then I continued toward home.

We live on a very quiet dead-end street. Mom and Dad like that, but sometimes it gets a little eerie because of the giant trees that line both sides of the road. They block the streetlights and cast long shadows. Four of those trees are in our front yard. They make our front porch pretty dark.

I walked past the trees. I thought I saw something move around the side of the house. If we had a dog or a cat, I might have thought it was our pet. But all I have is a goldfish, and it doesn't usually go out at night for walks.

I kept walking toward the house. I was a little unnerved, but I figured my eyes were playing tricks on me.

When I was halfway to the door, I heard a crash behind the house. It could have been something simple and logical. Dad could have been dropping the trash into the garbage can.

I tried to convince myself, but I felt a shiver of fear. I started singing a Petra tune to bolster my courage.

I reached the porch on shaky legs. As I breathed a sigh of relief, something touched me from behind.

I felt long tentacles brushing against my head and neck. I also felt the panic rise up from my stomach and form a lump in my throat.

I twisted to my right and lunged, leaping toward the front door. But I misjudged the distance and hit the door with a loud crash. I caught my balance just in time to keep from landing in a crumpled heap.

As I steadied myself, I looked over my shoulder to see what kind of creature had attacked me. And I came face to face with the branch of a large tree. It was swaying peacefully in the gentle breeze.

I had been "attacked" by a tree! I guess it was after my carbon dioxide.

I leaned against the door and laughed at my carbon dioxide joke. Suddenly the door swung open. I tumbled through the opening.

"Your mom and I wondered when you'd get home," Dad said after he recovered from jumping out of my way.

I stared up from the foyer floor and greeted him. "Hi, Dad. Just thought I'd drop in."

He chuckled and said, "Mom thought she heard some sort of animal at the front door. I came to check it out—and it looks like there *was* some sort of animal at the front door."

Dad reached down and pulled me to my feet. I snatched up my backpack, which had dropped from my shoulder, and followed him into the living room. I dropped my pack into a chair near the stairs as Dad said, "Tell me about soccer practice. Did you work on passing skills?"

"Practice went okay," I answered. "Coach had us doing the same drills over and over today. He pretty much wore us out."

Dad always asked about my activities. I felt pretty lucky to have a dad who cared so much about my life.

Turning toward the kitchen, he called through the house to Mom, "Katherine, you'll never believe what I found on our front porch."

"Let me guess. Is his name MacKenzie?" she called back. When we got to the kitchen, she had popped my dinner in the microwave and poured me a glass of milk.

"I called Spookie the Clown's Halls of Pizza today," she said. "Everything is set for Friday night from 8:00 to 10:00 P.M. I also called Coach Reese and Pastor Daniels. They agreed to help get the word out. Between the three of us, everyone should know where to meet on Friday."

"Thanks, Mom," I said. Mom and Dad had already eaten, so I sat quietly thinking about ghosts while I ate. When I finished, I put my plate in the dishwasher and headed toward my room.

I wanted to get to bed early. Tomorrow I had a meeting in the school library before classes. Several of us wanted to start a new book club. We all like to read scary stories, so we decided to meet and talk about our favorites. We even planned to loan some of our own books to each other.

I got to the bottom of the stairs and picked my backpack up off the chair where I'd left it. The light in the upstairs hallway was off, and the stairs reached up into darkness. My thoughts instantly returned to ghosts, and I actually hesitated on the bottom step.

I'm going to be twelve. I shouldn't be afraid of the dark up there. Right, Lord? I thought. But what I thought and what I felt were two very different things.

I realized my fear was silly and started to climb the steps. My mouth felt dry, and I could barely swallow. My heart beat as if I had just run a mile. I don't like the dark to begin with, and tonight my mind was running wild with pictures of ghosts in pizza parlors.

At the top of the stairs, I gripped the banister.

Of course, nothing reached out of the dark hallway and grabbed me. Nothing ever did.

I stretched my hand over to turn on the lamp—just like I did every night. Then I hustled down the hall to my room and pushed the door open.

As I entered, I glanced up at the window in my room. I stifled a cry, jumped back into the hall, and dropped my backpack with a crash.

Two huge eyes had been staring at me.

"What happened, MacKenzie?" my dad asked with concern from the bottom of the stairs.

"My backpack slipped from my hand," I answered. "Sorry to startle you." I told him only part of the story. I wasn't ready to tell him about the eyes until I checked them out myself.

I cautiously reached in and flipped on the light in my room. My eyes went immediately to the big window. Taped to it was a round yellow smiley face with huge eyes. Above it was a small banner that said HAPPY BIRTHDAY.

I laughed to myself. Mom had decorated my room with streamers and mobiles that all said HAPPY BIRTHDAY. My mom was crazy sometimes. I'd have to give her a thank-you hug in the morning.

After another look around, I shook my head and snickered. I stashed my backpack. Then I got my pajamas out of a drawer. I felt tired and sore from the long soccer practice.

After washing up and brushing my teeth, I sank deep under the covers, wanting to sleep. But the smiley-face scare had jarred me awake. I needed something to relax me.

Digging through the books I had ready for tomorrow morning's meeting, I found one that I had enjoyed years ago. I settled in to begin reading when I suddenly remembered the library book that I'd brought home. It was in my backpack.

I dug the heavy volume out of the bottom of the pack and set it on my bed. It wasn't exactly what I would call light reading. The book must have weighed two to three pounds.

For a moment, I had second thoughts about cracking open the book. Did I really want to know right now about the ghosts at Spookie's pizza place? After all, I wanted to get a good night's sleep.

But I knew the ghosts weren't real. So, just like Curious George, the monkey from some of my favorite books, I decided to see what I could discover. I stretched out on top of the covers and leaned back on my pillow. Then I pulled the big book up and rested it on my body. It fell open to chapter 13.

I hadn't even started to read before I recognized the fear overcoming me. *Lord?* I prayed. *I know there's no truth in these stories. Please help me to overcome my fear.* As I took in a deep breath, I felt a little bit calmer. I began reading where Lisa had left off that afternoon:

24

In the last fifty years, the large red-brick building that sits in the middle of Tremble Avenue's business district has seen more than thirty tenants. Many of the tenants and customers witnessed strange, unexplainable disturbances.

In the 1940s, mysterious sightings of a gaunt gray figure occurred. At that time the building housed Dandy's Five and Dime Store.

In one instance, a customer had selected her items from one of the basement bargain areas and walked to the register. Without looking up, she placed her purchases on the checkout counter. While she rummaged in her purse for money, the items moved off the counter, and the register rang.

The customer looked up expecting to see a clerk. But all she saw was the long kitchen knife she had selected. It was floating in midair. When she screamed, the knife dropped to the floor, and she heard a haunting, eerie laugh.

Big deal, I thought, still trying to dismiss my fears. *The woman probably needed to buy glasses instead of a kitchen knife. Besides, that happened before my dad was even born, and that was a long time ago.*

I debated with myself over whether I should read the rest of the chapter. I decided I was still curious, so I continued to read.

Over the years the building has changed hands many times. As of this writing, a new pizza restaurant for kids is planning to open after extensive remodeling. The previous owner ran a bakery that specialized in hand-decorated birthday cakes.

The bakery relocated because of recurring hauntings. In the final instance, one of the night shift bakers had gone to the basement for flour. The worker said that he was "attacked from behind. I didn't know what it was. I thought maybe a burglar had gotten in until these long, gray arms wrapped themselves around me. I struggled as hard as I could, and the two of us fell into the stacked bags of flour. Several of them broke, sending clouds of flour into the air. When it finally settled, I saw a thin, grayish-white form slipping into the next room."

The night baker said that he didn't follow the ghost but immediately ran upstairs and then outside, never to return to work on Tremble Avenue again.

I stopped reading for a moment and rubbed my eyes. It was getting hard to keep them open. I wanted a drink of water, but I didn't want to climb out of bed and get it. I was afraid of what I might encounter in the dark hall. I decided to stay in bed and try to relax. I breathed deeply and closed my eyes.

After a few minutes I picked up the book and began reading again.

The most recent unexplainable event at the Tremble Avenue building occurred on September 23 . . .

This year? On my birthday? Surely I misread that, I thought. I read the sentence again.

The most recent unexplainable event at the Tremble Avenue building occurred on . . .

I hadn't misread it. It was this Friday's date. I felt my breath come in shorter gasps as I read on.

MacKenzie Griffin, celebrating his twelfth birthday at Spookie the Clown's Halls of Pizza, mysteriously disappeared . . .

I dropped the book. My name! My birthday party! My pulse quickened, and I concentrated hard to keep from shaking. *Calm down, Mac. Your imagination is in overdrive. You didn't really read what you thought you just read.*
I returned to where I had left off.

Witnesses to the event reported strange

27

occurrences. Barry Lennon, Griffin's best friend, reported that a gray ghostlike being had cornered the young man in the basement.

Beads of perspiration broke out on my forehead.

"I closed my eyes out of fear," Lennon reported. "When I opened them again, MacKenzie was gone." MacKenzie Griffin is still missing . . .

Tears welled in my eyes. I could not explain what was happening.

Either I was going crazy, or this was some kind of phantom book that predicted the future.

A piercing wail shattered the silence. I jolted upright in my bed. The back of my pajama shirt was soaked with sweat and stuck to my skin.

Outside the wail grew fainter.

My mind cleared, and I recognized the sound as an ambulance siren. I rubbed my eyes.

Unbelievable! I had fallen asleep and dreamed I was reading about my birthday disappearance.

Mom must have turned off my reading lamp before going to bed. I turned it on again and reached for *Middletown's Ghosts and Ghouls,* which lay on the floor.

I opened the book and scanned chapter 13 with relief. No mention of my birthday party. In fact, the last sighting the book reported had happened a full year ago.

I placed the volume on my bedside table, turned out the light, and crawled under the covers. I prayed I wouldn't dream anymore.

On awaking the next morning, I hoped that lunch, school, homework, and bedtime would be more sane than my dream. I really needed to get my imagination under control.

After breakfast, I gathered up some of my scary book collection and headed for school. Several of us involved in forming the new book club walked into the library together. The lights were on, but no librarian was in sight. We sat down at the largest table.

I placed my collection in front of me. The others did the same. I looked over the stack next to mine. One kid brought a series for younger kids called *Boo! Books*.

While we waited for the librarian to come help us start our meeting, I said, "It looks like there are dozens of scary series. I'm not sure I've read many books in any of them. Maybe we should each give a short review on our favorites to start."

A girl from my math class said, "I thought they were all the same. Aren't they all about ghosts or monsters?"

The girl next to her responded, "No, my favorite books have historical backgrounds."

"One series I like is more about ghosts than monsters, and another is about a street called Scare Avenue," the boy across from me said.

"My favorites all have endings that will shock you. They've actually helped me deal with my fears," another boy added.

The boy across from me was just opening his mouth to say something else when the doors to the library flew open. Startled by the noise, I whipped my head around.

In the library's doorway stood a creature that looked like it had just climbed out of a grave.

We jumped from our seats and ran to the far corner of the library. The creature turned toward us, staring and moaning. Then it lurched in our direction.

I felt my heart beating in my throat. I had hoped today would be uneventful. Wrong.

We spread out along the back wall. The creep might be able to grab one or two of us, but some would be able to get away to get help. The refugee from the graveyard took a few more steps and twisted its head toward the table.

Our books diverted the thing's attention. It walked to a chair, pulled it out, and sat down. Slimy fingers reached out and grabbed one of my books and flipped it open.

We stood, shocked, watching the walking dead become the reading dead. The creature turned, stared at us, and spoke for the first time. "Good books."

Then the undead looked right at me and said,

"Mr. Griffin, if you can get your cohorts to sit down, I'd like to get started."

Suddenly, I recognized her voice—the librarian! Wow! Who would have expected the school librarian to do something so cool?

"I can't believe it's you," I said. "Why did you dress up to scare us?"

"That's simple. I dressed up like this because I wanted you to have a real experience that you can carry to your books. When you read, remember how you felt a few minutes ago. Such feelings help make stories come to life," she answered.

I didn't need her entrance to experience fright. I had pizza hall ghosts, floating raincoats, trees, and smiley faces to draw on for feelings of mouth-drying fear.

"That was really great," one of the other kids said.

"You should see what I do when classes study the ocean. Sea monsters are tough costumes to find, and seaweed isn't easy to clean up," she said as she smiled.

We gathered around her. She liked our idea about reviewing the different series. We decided which books to talk about at the next meeting. Then the bell rang, and we split up to start our classes.

The day passed quickly. Even soccer practice breezed by. When I walked out of the locker room into the late afternoon sun, I saw Lisa waiting for me beneath the big elm tree.

"What's going on? Why are you still here?" I quizzed.

Usually, Lisa and Frankie hang out together after school. I felt uneasy when I saw Lisa alone. Her expression concerned me even more.

"It's Davis," Lisa answered in a troubled tone. She looked frightened by something.

"What's wrong with Davis? Did he get hurt or something?" My words fairly flew out of my mouth as I quickly walked closer.

"He's all right now, but in a few minutes he may not be," Lisa said.

Lisa hadn't told me anything concrete, but she had managed to frighten me. My confusion and fear came out in my voice as I said, "Tell me what's going on. This suspense has to be worse than whatever is going to happen to Davis."

"When Frankie, Davis, and I were helping the biology teacher after school today, Davis started asking us lots of questions about Spookie's.

"We told him what we read in that library book yesterday, and he decided to have a look at that old building for himself. He left about ten minutes ago," Lisa stated.

"So, he'll walk by it, and it will look like a pizza place. Then he'll go home. What's the big deal?" I said to calm her fears for our friend, though my stomach was growing queasy with nervousness.

35

"That isn't exactly what he planned," Lisa continued. "He said he wants to disprove the legend before the party. He plans to get inside."

"I don't think there's anything to worry about," I said, trying to sound convincing to both Lisa and myself.

Lisa looked at me hard and said, "You're not listening to me, Mac. Davis plans to go around behind the building and find a way to get down to the basement. I told him it was a dumb idea, but Davis is trying so hard to be a part of our group. Sometimes, like now, I think he tries too hard."

My thoughts were racing. Surely, Davis would be safe in broad daylight. The restaurant workers and the early dinner crowd would be there. And all the stories about ghosts were just fiction, weren't they?

But what about the people I had read about—the people who had witnessed the apparitions, the baker who had been attacked by a ghost? Or what if someone thought Davis was a burglar?

"We've got to get down there and stop him," I said. "Hurry." I bolted past Lisa, grabbing her hand to drag her along as I ran toward Spookie the Clown's Halls of Pizza.

The restaurant was only a few blocks from the school. We could get there in five minutes. But Davis was probably already there. He could be in the hands of a ghost for all I knew.

We reached the building and stopped abruptly. I stared at the rough red-brick front. A large mural painted above the door showed an enormous clown's face. Out of his mouth came a dialogue balloon, like in comic books, saying, "Spookie the Clown's Halls of Pizza is a killer-fun place."

I wished I hadn't read that. I turned to Lisa and said, "Davis may already be inside. We need to do something quick to save him."

Stepping back from the building, I thought about how Davis might have gone in. It didn't seem likely that he'd use the front door if he wanted to get into the basement. Someone would probably stop him. To the left of the building was a narrow walkway that led to the back of the building.

Lisa looked at me with wide, frightened eyes and said, "He said something about going in the back door. He must have gone down that way. We better follow him."

"No, we can't both go. I'll go alone. You stay here and be the lookout. If I don't come back soon, call my parents, I told her.

I didn't *want* to go by myself. I really wanted Lisa to come with me, but if I didn't return, I wanted Lisa to go for help. I had to do this by myself. I knew it, but I didn't like it.

As I moved slowly down the narrow walkway, I wanted to sing or whistle. But if Davis needed rescuing, I couldn't make any noise and give myself away. Instead I prayed a silent prayer for our safety.

At the end of the walkway I found myself in a narrow alley that ran behind the buildings in this block. The stores and restaurants kept their garbage cans back there, out of sight.

I forced myself to walk toward Spookie's back door. Each step brought me closer, but my legs were heavy and my feet fought me when I lifted them.

When I was about a foot from the door, I heard someone turn the knob. I quickly searched for a place to hide. I was close enough to get behind the garbage dumpster before the door opened. I took one big leap and ducked down.

Someone came out and headed toward the dumpster I had hidden behind. I heard the lid open and two huge bags drop in. Then the lid slammed shut. In another few seconds, the back door closed.

I sighed and stood up. I took one step forward and almost tripped on my shoelace. As I reached down to tie my shoe, I saw Davis's prized Pittsburgh Pirates baseball cap. I snatched it off the ground.

My heart began beating out of control. Davis must have gotten inside!

I raced down the walkway toward Lisa holding Davis's cap in front of me.

Lisa saw me coming and then looked at the hat in my hands. She covered her mouth with her hands and let out a groan of fear. She took a step back and leaned against a streetlight.

"I found this by the back door. Davis must have gone inside. We've got to help him," I told her.

"What can we do?" Lisa asked, holding tightly to the lightpole.

"Let's go home. I'll call Barry, and you call Frankie. We need every one of our crew to come back tonight. We've got to help Davis. Plan to meet me here after dinner," I said.

We ran to our houses. I crashed through the front door, dropped my backpack by the staircase, and rushed into the kitchen where Dad was cooking dinner. "Dad, can Barry sleep over tonight?" I asked.

39

"Hey, is that any way to greet your old dad, especially when he's sweating over a hot stove?" Dad grinned at me.

"Sorry. Hi, Dad," I said. "Now, can Barry sleep over?"

Dad looked at me and raised his eyebrows while he thought. "I guess so. Why don't you go make sure it's okay with your mother?"

After I checked with Mom, I called Barry.

"Hi, Barry," I said. "This is Mac. I don't have time to explain right now, but somebody's got Davis. Ask your parents if you can sleep over so we can get into Spookie's to help him."

Barry's folks said okay. He promised to come over after dinner.

I tried to keep the conversation on school and soccer as I ate with my parents. I didn't want them to ask questions about Spookie's or my party. I was afraid I'd let something about Davis slip. I had gotten him into this mess, and I had to get him out—or so I thought.

As I was rinsing off the last dish from dinner, the doorbell rang. The next thing I knew, Barry was standing next to me with an intensely worried look on his face. He asked quietly, so my parents wouldn't hear, "What's going on, Mac?"

I quickly told him about the book, the legend of the clowns, the treasure, and what Davis had planned

40

on doing. Then I pulled Davis's Pirates cap from my back pocket. I told him how I had found the cap behind the haunted pizza place.

Barry said very little. He was not often so quiet. When I finished, he asked, "So, what's the plan?"

"We've got to check out Spookie's basement tonight. We're going to meet Frankie and Lisa. Once we're inside we'll split into pairs and search for Davis," I answered.

After I finished putting the dishes in the dishwasher, Barry and I headed upstairs so I could grab a jacket. We were almost to the top step when the phone rang. Mom answered it.

I ignored the call until I heard Mom say, "Sure, let me call him to the phone. I'm sure he can help you out."

Barry and I exchanged a worried look. What had Mom promised I would do? We had to go meet the girls now.

"MacKenzie, the phone is for you," Mom called up to me.

"See if I can call back, Mom. Barry and I are really busy," I responded.

"Mac, it's Davis Wong. He says he really needs your help," she said.

Davis Wong? I suddenly had to sit down.

"Are you going to get it upstairs, Mac?" Mom asked.

"Yes, I'll get it in my room."

I stood up and raced Barry down the hall to my room. I snatched up the phone and said, "Thanks, Mom, I've got it."

I waited for her to hang up and whispered into the phone, "Davis, this is Mac. I know where you are, and we're planning to come over to get you out of there."

"What are you talking about?" Davis responded. "I'm at home watching TV. Why would I want you to come and get me out of my house?"

"Well, I thought that . . . oh, never mind." A big smile of relief spread across my face. So Barry would know what was going on, I asked, "How did you get out?"

"Out of what? Mac, what happened? Did you get hit on the head at soccer practice?" he quizzed.

"Didn't you go to Spookie's after school?"

Davis laughed and responded, "Sure, and that's why I'm calling. I went down the walkway next to the building and found the back door. I was going to sneak in, but someone came out, and I ran out of there. The only trouble is that I dropped my Pirates cap somewhere. I was wondering if you could go with me before school to look for it."

"Davis, I'll do even better than that. I went looking for you and found your cap. I'll bring it to school tomorrow," I answered.

Barry was almost jumping up and down as I got off the phone. He wanted to know what had happened. After I told him, I called Frankie and Lisa.

Later, Barry and I worked on our homework for a little while. Then I dug out one of my favorite video games and challenged Barry. I thought that since I had the home court advantage, I could win. I should have known better. Video games are Barry's thing. He beats me every time.

"How do you do that? Do you practice every day?" I asked in frustration.

"You know that I play almost every day, but I also seem to have a gift for it," he answered.

"I don't think there's a gift or talent called Video Game," I challenged.

"No, that isn't the way I mean it. It takes a degree of concentration and eye-hand coordination. I just do these things well," he said. Then he sat back against

44

the foot of the bed. I could tell he was deep in thought.

"What are you thinking about?" I asked. "Are you scared that I'll beat you so badly that you won't be able to show your face at school?" I asked, joking around.

He hesitated. Do you think ghosts really exist?" he asked.

I sat back against the bed too. "Well, I do know that Ephesians 6:12 says, 'We are fighting against the rulers and authorities and the powers of this world's darkness.' And God's Spirit is greater than the darkness. So I guess that if there *are* ghosts there's really nothing to be afraid of."

We sat quietly until the wind moved a branch, and it brushed against my window. "Did you hear that?"

"It was just the wind, I think," he answered.

Funny how I could quote Scripture and still be spooked a minute later. My imagination had started to run away with even the smallest things. I was getting tired, and my mind always played tricks on me when I got tired. "I think we better hit the hay," I told him.

"Hit the what?" he asked in confusion.

"Hit the hay. It means 'go to bed,'" I told him. I thought everyone used that expression.

"Why does it mean 'go to bed'? Where do you suppose that expression comes from?" Barry pondered.

"Listen, I've already used up all my brain power on the plan to free Davis. Let's get some sleep and ask someone else in the morning."

We laughed and got ready for bed. I had two beds in my room, so I could have friends over. Barry used my spare bed more than anyone else I knew.

I had just started to drift off to sleep when I heard a crash from the backyard.

I slipped out of bed and shook Barry, but he was already awake.

"Hey, did you hear that?" I asked. "I heard the same thing yesterday when I was coming home from the library."

"Yes, I heard something like it around my house last night too," he answered. "My mom sent Dad out to see what caused it, but he didn't find anything. If we could figure out what's making the noise, my mom would sleep a whole lot better. Let's check it out. . . . Or do you think it might be ghosts?"

I gave him my don't-be-ridiculous look, and we slipped out of our beds. I opened the door slowly. My parents were already in bed. It was quiet and dark downstairs.

I crept down the stairs as Barry stayed close behind me. We tiptoed past Mom and Dad's bedroom door and into the kitchen. I silently twisted the knob and pulled the back door open. We slipped silently outside into the dark night.

"Where do you think the noise came from?" my best friend whispered.

"I couldn't tell, but let's try near the garbage cans," I told him. As we crept toward the cans, we heard a noise. We spun ourselves around to face the garage.

Barry motioned to me to keep silent. Together we crept softly through the wet grass. I couldn't see anything by the small building.

As we got closer, something moved in the bushes in front of us. We looked at each other and I gulped. I thought, *Is it really a ghost? Is it one of the 'powers of this world's darkness'?*

Another four steps put us next to the big bush. I searched near the ground. Barry let out a howl. I looked up as a dark form leaped at Barry's head from the bush.

Barry dived for the ground as the ghostly figure flew toward his head. It missed him by only two inches, but it didn't miss me.

"Help! Get it off me!" I cried out.

I twisted and turned in a wild attempt to free myself from the sharp claws of the phantom. I finally grabbed its head, and it hissed and growled.

A black cat decided I had scared it enough. It let go of my chest, dropped to the wet grass by my feet, and shot off into the night.

Barry had seen the terror in my eyes. Then he saw the cat and cracked up.

"Did the little kitty scare you?" he asked.

"At least I stayed on my feet," I fired back.

We both broke out in giggles as the tension eased out of us. Finally I got my breath back and said, "We better get back to bed before our little adventure wakes Mom and Dad."

We didn't say anything as we crossed the lawn and

climbed the back porch steps. As I pulled the screen door open, a sinking feeling hit my stomach. I had forgotten to turn the button to keep the door from locking behind us.

I grabbed the knob and tried twisting it. Nothing happened. We were locked out.

"I've got some bad news," I told my friend. "We locked ourselves out of the house."

"Then we'll just go around to the front door and ring the bell. Your dad will open the door, and we'll all go back to bed," he answered simply.

"Barry, I've had a tough enough time convincing them that I can be responsible. If they find out I did something stupid like locking myself out over a silly cat, they'll treat me like a little kid until I'm old enough for my beard to reach my navel."

"How about a window?" he suggested.

"That's a good idea. Dad usually leaves the one in his workroom open. He likes lots of fresh air. I'll bet he didn't lock it the last time he was in there," I said as I ran around to the side of the house.

The window was wide open. I bent over to inspect it. It would be tough to get through, but I thought we could. By then Barry was standing behind me.

"Maybe my first idea was better. Let's go around front and ring the bell," he suggested strongly.

I lay down flat on the ground. Technically, I guess I lay down right on top of Dad's prize flowers. I attempted to move them out of the way, but a good bed of flowers is hard to move. I'd have to tell my parents the whole story in the morning. But at least they'd get an uninterrupted night's sleep first.

I wiggled in through the window. Dad's workbench stood directly below the window. The drop was short, but Dad had left a glass jar of nuts and bolts near the edge. In the dark, I bumped it.

Nothing I did could stop its suicide leap to the floor. The crash of breaking glass and scattering metal sent shivers through me.

I tried to keep Barry from knocking anything else off the bench. But he kicked a mallet, and it toppled off. I could barely see it as my hand shot into the darkness to stop its fall. I snatched it out of the air.

We stood in the workroom. "If any ghouls got in here before us, I'll bet they're waiting for us in the rec room," I said in a very low whisper.

"Do you think they came in so they could play foosball?" Barry joked.

I ignored him. Before I could open the door, I heard movement on the other side.

"What should we do?" Barry asked, his eyes wide.

"I don't know. Maybe we should grab a hammer and go after it," I answered.

"We don't have to go after it. It's coming to us!" Barry said in panic as he watched the knob turn slowly.

The door flew open.

"DAD!" I screamed as he began to swing a base-ball bat in the air.

He stopped mid swing, reached over, and flipped on the light. Dad stared at us in surprise. Then he sucked in a deep breath and set the bat down.

"Could you please explain to me why you're sneaking into the house through my workroom window? And while you're at it, I'd like to know why you were outside in the first place. And don't you realize that it's dangerous to break into a house? I could have really hurt you. I thought you were thieves," he said, his anger rising as he realized what we'd done.

"It was really stupid, Mr. Griffin, but it was my idea." Barry attempted to take the blame.

"Thanks, Barry, but this is my house. I knew the rules, and I broke them. I'm sorry, Dad. We heard something crash, and we slipped outside to see what it was. But instead of finding some ghoul strolling around the garden, we locked ourselves out."

"You heard it too?" Dad said with interest. He seemed to forget he was mad at us. He totally refocused on the mysterious noise. "Did you see anything?"

"We heard something by the garage. When we went to investigate, a cat jumped on me."

"Hmm. Why don't we get some sleep and talk in the morning?" Dad suggested.

As we walked upstairs, he said, "You two can sleep in an extra fifteen minutes. I'll drive you to school."

When morning came, I expected crazy things to happen at school after all the excitement of the last few days, but it was rather dull until lunchtime.

Barry described to our friends how we'd confronted a horrible ghoul in my backyard. I liked his version. We sounded much braver than we'd been.

Frankie looked him right in the eyes and said, "I don't believe this story."

"It's true," Barry defended.

"Most of it is true," I added.

"Which part is true?" Davis asked.

"We did see a mysterious, dark shape that looked like a ghost in the backyard," I answered.

"I saw a ghost in my pajamas once," Davis said with a smile. "What he was doing in my pajamas, I'll never know."

Frankie and Lisa laughed so hard they nearly fell from their cafeteria seats. Barry and I were not amused.

I opened my lunch bag and pulled out my sandwich. When I unwrapped it, the bread had "Happy Birthday, Almost" written on it in mustard. *Thanks Mom,* I thought.

"Cute—really cute," Frankie said. "I can't wait to see what the rest of your lunch looks like."

Lucky for me Mom hadn't gotten too creative this morning. The rest of the school day seemed to slip by.

That evening, before I went into the house, I checked where we'd seen the cat by the garage. I wanted to make sure we hadn't missed something. I didn't find any clues. Maybe all the noise just came from the cat. Next, I made sure the window to Dad's workroom was closed. Assured that nothing could get in, I went inside.

I discovered that Mom and Dad were still at work. I looked around for anything unusual. I knew I was starting to get paranoid. It was crazy to think that ghosts would be lurking around the house waiting for me. I decided to think less about ghosts and more about the protector *against* ghosts.

The rest of my last evening as an eleven-year-old was completely uneventful. I hoped the beginning of my twelfth year would be as well.

I got up early on my birthday, showered, and dressed. I was pulling on my Dodgers cap as I stepped into the silent kitchen. Where were Mom and Dad? Then I noticed my spot at the table. A tower of pancakes just about glowed—twelve candles burned happily on top.

My parents leaped out from behind the kitchen counter yelling, "Happy Birthday!"

"Thanks, Mom and Dad. I can't believe that I'm twelve, almost a full-grown man." I threw that in as a hint to my mother.

"Hurry and blow out the candles," Dad said.

"Okay, please let my party tonight be the talk of the school on Monday," I wished. I puffed out the candles with a single blow.

The pancakes were great, and I was only halfway through when Barry showed up at the back door to walk to school with me.

"Wow!" he said as he peeked through the screen door. "That's the biggest pile of pancakes I've ever seen."

"You know how it is when you're the birthday boy," I said with a grin. I took a few more bites, grabbed my backpack, and we were on our way to school.

It was a quiet morning, but I knew lunch wouldn't be as quiet. Tonight was my party at Spookie's. I imagined we'd probably meet up with whatever was haunting that building. I was sure we'd talk about it while we ate.

At lunchtime, I walked into the cafeteria and sat at an empty table. Barry and Frankie arrived next from their class together. I saw Lisa in the lunch line beside Davis.

Since Davis's dad was the vice principal, they felt he should eat the sometimes mysterious cafeteria food. Vice Principle Wong wanted to emphasize how good the food could be. But it wasn't.

"How are the party plans for tonight, MacKenzie?" Frankie asked.

"Just about everyone I invited is coming. To tell you the truth, after all the strange things that have happened this week, I have a feeling that tonight may be the weirdest night of my life," I told the others.

Lisa agreed, but Frankie didn't believe it would be scary. She told us, "A girl in my English class said her little brother had a party there last week and nothing unusual happened. No one saw any type of ghoul, ghost, or phantom. I think we're all getting a little carried away with the legend about the Tremble Avenue building."

But Davis insisted, "I heard just the opposite. A couple of guys from gym class said it was definitely haunted and that two kids went in and never came out last week. The police don't want to panic anyone, so nothing's been in the news about their disappearance."

"It doesn't matter what anyone's saying. Tonight, we'll all find out for ourselves," Barry told us.

I opened my lunch bag and pulled out my sandwich. Then I dumped out an apple and a bag of chips. A brightly wrapped gift fell onto the table from the bottom of my bag. The others looked at me.

"Open it," Frankie urged.

"Mom didn't say anything about a birthday gift in my lunch bag. How do I know it's from her? It could be from anybody, including the ghosts at Spookie's," I kidded, using my best scary voice.

I took the bow off the package. "Well, nothing happened—so far."

I undid a piece of tape on the bottom. "It still didn't blow up," I joked some more.

Then I ripped the Happy Birthday wrapping paper off the small box. "Nothing unusual," I said, stretching out the suspense.

"Well, are you going to open the box or not?" Frankie asked.

"Would you open a gift some ghost sneaked into your lunch bag?" Lisa said.

I wasn't sure if she were kidding or not. I looked at her face for a clue.

"Of course," she continued, "if some loving, caring ghost took the time to wrap a nice gift to make my birthday a little brighter, I'd open it a lot faster than Mac is." Then she started laughing.

I smiled and pulled the top off the box.

"Oh, no!" I gasped.

"HAPPY BIRTHDAY! HAPPY BIRTHDAY! HAPPY BIRTHDAY! HAPPY BIRTHDAY! HAPPY BIRTHDAY! HAPPY BIRTHDAY! HAPPY BIRTHDAY!" a computer chip blared.

Everyone in the entire cafeteria stood up to see what was going on. Some kids even climbed on chairs to get a better look.

I didn't know what to do. My first instinct was to put the lid back on the box. But I couldn't find it. I must have dropped it on the floor. I stuck my head beneath the table to look for it. I sort of wanted to just stay under the table. Then the sound stopped as suddenly as it had begun.

I crawled out from under the table and found myself the focus of a roomful of stares. I smiled sheepishly. I was embarrassed, but I also felt the urge to giggle. I looked at everyone and asked, "Does anyone else have a birthday gift for me?" People started laughing and went back to their lunches.

We didn't have soccer practice today, so after school, I hurried home to tell Mom about the havoc she had caused, but she had gone out. She left me a note on the fridge that said she'd gone shopping for party favors. I could see her coming home with brightly colored little bags with plastic whistles, lollipops, and fake watches. I shook my head and decided to shoot a few hoops to burn off some of my pre-birthday-party excitement.

I got into a zone, hitting my shots one after another—nothing but net. I was so into shooting that I didn't realize Mom came home. Then I heard her call out my name, "MacKenzie, we need to get going, or you'll be late for your own birthday party."

I rolled the ball into the garage and headed for the minivan. Mom had already thrown things for the party into the back. For a long time, I'd told her that since I was an only child, she could get a sportier car. She sort of took my advice; she got a *red* minivan.

She picked up Barry, Davis, Frankie, and Lisa. Everyone else would meet us at Spookie's. I had invited kids from three different groups. There were the guys I played soccer with, my best friends in the van with me, and other kids from my church youth group. It should be a pretty big turnout.

We wanted to be the first to get there. Mom pulled to a stop in front of Spookie's as a bunch of little kids were leaving the Halls of Pizza. Their party must have just ended. They all had bright helium balloons stringing from their wrists and traditional birthday bags of goodies in their hands.

I sighed. None of them looked scared; Spookie's really must be a place for little kids. I wouldn't be able to show my face at school, practice, or church. How much fun could this be for a bunch of middle schoolers if little kids looked unfazed? *This is going to be a drag,* I thought.

We all jumped out. I had taken only a few steps from the minivan when Barry stopped me. "Afraid to go in?" I asked. "Maybe you're afraid you'll lose at pin the tail on the donkey."

"Yeah, right. I just wanted to tell you I read something in the newspaper about this place," he said seriously.

"So?"

"This building really is haunted. It's like the Bermuda Triangle of town. Strange things happen here. The article talked about the last business to go under and the one before that. I asked my dad about it, and he said there are supposedly ghosts here looking for hidden treasure," he whispered.

"That's the legend," I told him.

"I'm not sure I want to go in . . . , but I'm not staying out here by myself," he finished, and we walked in.

Mom checked in with Spookie while I greeted my guests as they came through the door. We were told to wait in the Halls of Pizza foyer until everyone had arrived. The foyer's walls were covered with all kinds of crazy things. It looked a lot cooler than I thought it would.

On one wall was a stuffed clown head. Kind of like those moose heads people hang on their walls as trophies.

I nudged Davis and said, "Tough place. They even stuff the heads of dead clowns. Or do you think the ghosts did that to him? Maybe he got too close to the treasure and they put an end to him."

Frankie looked up and pointed at the stuffed head on the wall. She said, "My dad wants one of those with a purple dinosaur on it."

Davis and I cracked up. It helped me to forget what Barry had reminded me of.

We continued making jokes about the clown's head. Suddenly it opened its eyes and yelled, "Welcome to Spookie the Clown's Halls of Pizza."

I jumped back and nearly knocked Lisa over. I heard my friends let out gasps and little shrieks. My heart leaped into my mouth, and I felt totally speechless.

Spookie pulled his head through a hole in the wall, and we heard him drop to the floor on the other side with a thump. When he opened a door, I saw several clown servers standing just beyond him. He said, "Hey, kids. Welcome to my Halls of Pizza. Are you ready to have a fun and crazy evening with us? We've got some really wacky games and loony prizes. Ho, hey, ho! This is going to be one fun-n-n-n night!"

I rolled my eyes and shot a glance at the kids around me. "I knew it was really him all the time," I told them.

Frankie and Lisa giggled. I guess they didn't believe me.

Spookie came over, grabbed my arm, and ushered me and my friends to the door. I was surprised when

I looked into the next room. The place was enormous and filled with video games. One wall had several doors marked Hall of this and Hall of that. I stood there taking it all in as the games beeped, whirred, gasped, and dinged only a few feet away.

The game room looked like a blast. I just hoped that Spookie and his clown team wouldn't make us sing little kids' songs or play baby games later in the party. If they did, I might crawl under a table and not come out until I graduated from middle school.

Spookie spun around, clapped his hands together, and said, "Boys and girls, can I have your attention?"

Everyone groaned in unison.

"Oops, did I say something wrong? You know Spookie, just kidding around. Anyway, children, please follow me and my fellow clowns into the party room."

We fell in behind the clown corps. The party room reminded me of a carnival midway. Games lined the sides of the room, and tables filled the center.

Spookie had gone all out for this place. Even the hologram characters near the midway games looked real. Of course, in the blinking, colored lights almost anything could have looked real. The lights cast an odd glow on everything.

We all wandered around as Spookie's clowns pushed chairs and tables into place. The holograms sang and danced.

In a dark corner, far from the entrance, a hologram depicted a group of kids playing a game of ring-around-the-rosy. They pranced in a circle around an odd figure. From the distance, in the crazy light, the figure in the center looked like a dingy gray sheet draped over something.

I walked closer to get a better look. When I got about five feet away, I found myself looking into its eyes. It wore a baggy clown costume, but it wasn't brightly colored like the other clowns. Instead, everything, including its skin, was gray. A shiver ran up my spine. Could this be one of the ghosts that haunted the Tremble Avenue building?

I shook my head to knock that frightening thought loose, then took a step back. I bumped into someone. One of the clowns?

Before I could turn around to look, the person behind me asked, "Do you know about the legend behind that scene?"

I tried to face the owner of the voice, but two hands gripped my shoulders, holding me still. "Do you? Do you know where the rhyme ring-around-the-rosy came from?"

I answered, "No, sir. I came over to see what the kids were dancing around . . ."

The person behind me didn't let me finish. He said, "When England was struck with the plague hundreds of years ago, people thought the dirty air

65

was killing them. So, they filled their pockets with flowers and walked around with handfuls of posies up to their noses. Don't you think it was silly of them to try to protect themselves with flowers?" He took his hands off my shoulders.

The creepy voice scared me so badly that my teeth started to chatter. I was too scared to turn around. When I tried to speak, my voice came out high and squeaky. "Uh, thank you for telling me about the rhyme. I guess you want me to join the others now?" I hoped I could escape this presence unharmed.

The voice didn't respond. Surprised, I spun around and discovered I was alone. Where did he go? I found myself beginning to buy into this ghost business. Had I just met one of them?

I didn't want to hang around and find out. I shot back toward my friends.

The others had already found places to sit around the tables. A large red velvet chair stood in the center of the room. I figured it was for me when Barry and Davis waved me over to it. They were sitting on either side of my birthday throne. Frankie and Lisa sat next to them, and the rest of my friends seemed to merge into a sea of faces.

Barry said something to me as I sat down, but the old-time organ music was so loud that I couldn't hear him. When I tried to yell into his ear that I had met a ghost, the music grew even louder.

66

The music didn't stop until Spookie joined us again and clapped his hands. It was obvious that he was the clown in charge.

"Throughout the evening, we will escort you to different areas for different activities. I see that we can split you easily into groups of five. Sometimes one group will be one place while the others are someplace else. Don't worry. We'll all end up in the same room when the party ends," he explained.

"That is, if the ghosts of Tremble Avenue don't get us first," Barry whispered to me.

"That's what I was trying to tell you. I went over to check out that gray figure in the middle of the kids playing ring-around-the-rosy, and a ghost grabbed me," I whispered back excitedly.

Barry looked at me and then glanced at the hologram. He asked, "What did the ghost look like?"

"I don't know. He grabbed me from behind, and when I turned around, he was gone. But he told me some weird tale about ring-around-the-rosy. He really spooked me," I told him in a loud whisper.

He scrunched his eyebrows together and looked like he wanted to ask me another question. But before he could open his mouth, clowns swarmed all around us with plates and glasses.

These clowns sure didn't look happy. Most had their faces painted in demented, angry, or twisted expressions. As my waitress reached over my shoulder to set down a glass, she looked right at me and snarled.

For a second I thought that maybe Spookie's wasn't just for little kids. Maybe it was going to be too much for me, even if I was practically an adult.

I leaned over to Davis to ask if he'd gotten a good look at the waitress's face. "Hey, did you see that? I don't think she's . . ."

CRASH! The wall across from us blew apart in a puff of smoke, sending stone fragments into the air. As the air cleared, I heard a horn beep. I couldn't believe it.

A car had smashed through the wall and was heading, out of control, directly toward our table.

14

My friends and I dived for the floor as tires screeched. The almost cartoonish-looking auto still slid toward us. The car's clown-faced driver's eyes were wide with what looked like terror.

I couldn't tell if she was terrified that she'd hit us or terrified that she'd miss us. It looked like she was steering deliberately at us.

"What's going on?" Davis yelled above the noise.

Lisa looked shocked as she screamed, "We've got to get out of here. That thing's still coming right at us."

We scrambled out of the way, just in time.

"It looks like my birthday party will be everybody's last party," I said to no one in particular. But I don't think anyone heard me above the screeching tires and screaming kids.

The car finally stopped. Thankfully no one got hit. The clown driver jumped out of her seat and yelled, "Howdy, am I late for the party?"

Spookie leaned on one of the tables, shaking with laughter. He could barely get the words out, "Look, kids! It's Penny the Party Crasher."

Penny had driven through a fake wall built out of plastic blocks. A smoke bomb made the explosion seem more realistic. I looked up and realized clown helpers had already begun to rebuild the wall.

After we all picked ourselves up and got back into our seats, Penny bounced from table to table doing silly magic tricks.

"Did I scare you kids?" she asked as we dug into our pizza.

"No, and we're not kids," I answered. I didn't want to give her the satisfaction of knowing that she'd just about terrified me.

She reached her white-gloved hand over and tousled my hair. Then Penny reached for my ear and produced some coins. She dropped them on the table, then reached for more. They just kept pouring out. Hundreds fell to the table as she giggled.

"Well, birthday boy, you really should clean your ears out more often," Penny said loudly. "You had all these tokens for Spookie's Hall of Games stuck inside your eardrum. But I beat them out of you. Get it? Beat them out? Eardrum? Beat drum?"

I understood her joke but didn't think it was very funny. Did she really think I'd believe she had pulled those coins out of my ear? I must have looked dubious because Penny snapped her fingers in front of my face.

"Hey, birthday boy, are you still with me?" she asked.

I smiled. "That was a great trick. Do you think if you looked harder you might find a handheld video game in there?" I joked. She smiled and moved on to another group of kids.

When the pizza had been devoured, Spookie whistled to get everyone's attention. Then he said, "Okay gang, it's time to head for the Hall of Games for a good time. That is, if MacKenzie will share the tokens Penny found in his ear."

I smiled as Spookie continued, "Try to stay in your groups of five. We're going to have a big surprise for some of you."

Spookie directed everyone to take a handful of tokens off the table in front of me. Then we all ran toward the game room. I went right to my favorite game, Guardians. Superhero angels fight with the bad guys who look like ghouls and ghosts. It's really cool. It's based on the characters from my favorite comic book series, also called Guardians.

Barry and I had all the editions. We both wanted to play the game, but he let me go first because it was my birthday and my favorite game.

I dropped in the tokens and reached for the start button—but the game began by itself. I didn't want to waste a second of playing time. I grabbed the joystick and started moving it while I pushed the weapons buttons.

I was racking up lots of points. I laughed at how good I was getting. I was in the video game zone.

Others started crowding around me. Someone accidentally pushed Davis, and he knocked my elbow. I momentarily lost my grip on the controls, but the game continued to play. It was as if something invisible had taken over the joystick.

The game was approaching the final level. I had gotten there only once before. There were so few of the Guardians video games around that I hadn't had much practice. I was almost afraid to tighten my grip on the controls again, but I didn't want to frighten the other kids.

I closed my fingers around the joystick. Even though it looked like I was playing great, I knew I wasn't controlling the game. Was it haunted? Several of the kids from school cheered as my score continued to climb.

I was about to make the highest score in my video game career, but something else had control over the game. I watched my score mount up. As I stared at the screen, I saw a shadow of a face slowly form over the graphics. It had a grayish tinge.

In fear, I recognized the face of the gray clown from the ring-around-the-rosy hologram. As the picture sharpened, I watched a hand with long, sharp nails move up near the face.

The horrible clown came into crystal-clear view and motioned for me to come closer. Then I heard a weird whisper: "Come and play with me. Come closer and play my game, but don't touch my treasure." I watched as flower petals dropped from the sharp-nailed hand and floated away.

I backed away from the game. Hadn't anyone else seen the face?

Barry slipped into my place and said, "Don't quit now. You're almost—ahhhhh!" Barry yelped off the end of his sentence as the face became visible to him. I guess you had to stand directly in front of the game to see it. He jumped back in surprise and landed on one of my feet.

"Ouch!" I yelled out in pain.

Everyone in the room looked at us. I saw Spookie lean close to Penny's ear and say something then snicker. I did not like the looks of that.

I turned back to the Guardians game, but the face had disappeared. All that was left was a frowning yellow circle of a face with the words, "Better luck next time," beneath it. I tried to shake off what I had seen as I pulled my group away from the video game.

I put my head close to Barry's so no one else would hear us.

"Did you see what I saw?" I asked.

"The face? That's not what I expected when you got to that level of the game," Barry answered.

I shook my head. "I don't think it had anything to do with the game. It was too real looking. Besides, I wasn't controlling the score at all. I even let go of the joystick, and the game continued on its own. I'm not sure I like this place anymore."

"Neither do I, especially after what you said was in that book you read," Barry added. Frankie and Davis interrupted us when they grabbed our arms and yanked us toward a booth called *The Game of Life*.

Lisa was standing in front of it reading something. She started instructing us, "According to these directions, we need to get inside the booth and sit down. Then we drop our tokens in the slot and grip the controls in front of us. Sounds easy enough."

I was about to tell them what had happened when Barry said, "After the last game, I could use something a little more sane."

Lisa pushed me into the seat. Lisa, Davis, Barry, and Frankie slid in beside me. We were firmly in place when Frankie dropped in the tokens.

The doors shut quickly, and a bar dropped over our laps. As we all instinctively put our hands on the bar, it locked tight across our knees. We were caught in *The Game of Life* as it began to flash and groan.

In front of us a large curved screen flicked on as loud music poured into the booth. *The Game of Life* flashed across the screen. We looked at one another.

I said, "This doesn't seem like some kind of kids' game to me. Spookie's place is starting to get to me. Barry, maybe we should tell them about Guardians."

Frankie said, "Relax, Mac, this is probably one of those virtual reality rides. It will look and feel like we're in a roller coaster or a spaceship or something."

A face appeared on the screen. As it came into focus, Frankie remarked, "Why is that clown face in black and white?"

I stared at the grayish clown face. "Barry, it's him! It's the face from ring-around-the-rosy and Guardians."

Before anyone could say another word, the ghostly clown spoke in an eerie, hollow voice: "Welcome to

The Game of Life. I'm your host, George Ghouless. Now, let's begin the game. The rules are simple. If you score enough points, we'll open the doors and let you out. And if you don't, we won't."

We tried to jump out, but the lap bar held us tight. We twisted and pulled up on the bar, but it was useless.

"What do we do?" Davis asked.

Lisa fairly hissed, "I guess we'd better answer the questions right. I don't want to end up as an eternal guest of Spookie's game room."

The creepy gray clown spoke again. "Here are your category choices: the History of European Wars, the Mammals of New Zealand, and Horror Movie Trivia. Which do you prefer?"

Barry answered for us all. "I don't think we have much choice. We haven't covered European history at school yet. I don't know much about New Zealand's mammals. Do you?" he asked as he looked at the rest of us.

When we shook our heads, he continued, "Right now, I wish Dracula were here to help us."

"I guess Horror Movie Trivia is my choice. What about you guys?" I asked.

Everyone agreed.

Our computer host said, "Horror Movie Trivia it will be then. Here is your first question: Who was the Bride of Frankenstein supposed to marry?"

I smiled. This might not be so hard. "That's easy," I said. "She was made for Frankie himself."

"Correct. Let's move to question two. What did Dracula sleep in, and what did it sit on?"

We all knew he slept in his coffin, but no one knew what it sat on. When we made several wild guesses, a horn buzzed so loud that our teeth rattled.

Our game host chimed in, "Dracula's coffin had to sit on dirt from his home in Transylvania. Are you ready for the third question?"

We all shook our heads, but the question came anyway: "What famous cartoon dog chased ghosts?"

"That one's easy," said Frankie. She broke out in the song, "Scooby-Dooby-Doo, where are you?"

"Correct," George Ghouless said. "One more correct answer, and I'll set you free. Two more incorrect answers, and you'll be locked inside forever. Question number four is: When does a werewolf come out?"

"At night," Barry yelled.

The horn buzzed again, so loud that it made us all jump.

"I think the questions are getting harder," I said to the others. "We better come up with the answer to the next question. By the way, werewolves come out only during a full moon."

Then George said, "Time for our last question. Answer it right, and you'll go free. Answer it wrong, and prepare to stay for a long time."

"Thanks for the encouragement," Frankie commented.

Lisa said, "We absolutely have to answer this one right."

I could hear panic in her voice. I realized that she felt the same way that I did.

"Attention!" George commanded. "Question number five:" he paused dramatically, "What did Dr. Jekyll turn into?"

Barry almost blurted out an answer, but I shot him a glance. "What are our choices?" I whispered to the others. I didn't want to say anything too loudly until we were sure. We couldn't afford to give another wrong answer.

"A monster," Davis let out quietly, as if one were breathing down his neck.

"An evil relative of the werewolf?" Lisa's high-pitched voice sounded unnatural.

"We don't have time to guess. The clock is ticking. Doesn't anyone know the real answer?" I pleaded.

Frankie thought for a moment then nearly shouted, "Mr. Hyde!"

George gave a ghoulish bark of laughter.

Had we won?

Had we lost?

The rest of us stared at Frankie. She had sealed our fate. Had she given the wrong answer?

Our host gave us a sinister smile as he reached for a switch. Instantly the door to our booth slid open, the bar across our knees lifted, and the seat tipped up, dumping us on the floor.

"Yes, Frankie! You saved us," I cried. "I'll live to see another birthday."

"Nothing to it," she said, but her eyes looked distracted.

A few feet away, five other guests were entering a booth similar to the one we had just escaped from. It was called *The Game of Chance.*

Frankie ran their way, but the group was already inside and the door was sliding shut.

"What should I do?" she asked, turning back to us.

"Try forcing the door open," Davis suggested.

By then Barry and I had joined Frankie next to *The Game of Chance.* Together we pressed hard on the door, and it slowly slid open. I expected to see five surprised faces. Instead, we found an empty booth.

"Where did they go?" Barry asked me.

I stuck my head inside the booth but found no sign of my friends. I looked carefully for a trapdoor, but the walls of the booth looked seamless. On the seat I noticed a few flower petals. I thought about the posies in the ring-around-the-rosy game. Had George Ghouless taken five of my friends?

I turned back to the others. "I don't see how they could have gotten out, but I found these."

Frankie looked confused and said, "Five people disappear and you're worried about flower petals?"

I started to tell them about the hologram, but Davis cut me off by saying, "We better tell Spookie."

Frankie gave him a hard, long look. "Don't you realize he's probably behind all this weird stuff? We can't tell Spookie."

The moment she mentioned his name, Spookie's voice blasted from the speaker above my head. "The Hall of Games time is over. Please follow my assistants to the Hall of Food."

Doors opened and several clowns escorted us into a room that looked like something out of the 1950s. The center of the room was empty and had an interesting black-and-white square patterned floor. Along one wall stood an old-fashioned counter with high red stools. Two sides of the room held red cushioned booths. Above the booths the walls were covered with mirrors. The fourth wall was draped in red velvet.

A tall, thin man wearing a white paper hat greeted us with, "Welcome to Big Rick's Cafe. Have a seat. In a few minutes we'll be having—"

Spookie interrupted by yelling over the noise we were making, "Before we have cake and ice cream, we're going to play some party games."

I said to the others, "He sure is rude. He didn't let Big Rick finish."

"Who?" Frankie turned to me and asked.

"He's right over there." I pointed to where Big Rick had been. No one was there. "I'm sure he was standing right there. I wonder where he went."

Barry gave me a puzzled look and said, "To leave the room, he'd have had to walk right through us to get to the door. That's the only exit."

He was right. I must have been seeing things, or . . . "Do you think it could have been a ghost?" I asked.

"I think you're getting delirious from too much pizza and too many flashing lights. Besides, we saw a bunch of little tykes leave this place. If they weren't scared, we shouldn't be either," Frankie said.

I was beginning to wonder if anything rattled my friend.

Frankie could have been right, but I was sure that I'd seen something.

As we gathered where Spookie had indicated, I looked around for the group that had gone into *The Game of Chance.* None of them were here.

Before I could comment to anyone, Spookie yelled again, "Quiet down, everyone. It's time for some traditional party games."

"Pin the tail on the donkey?" Davis asked. "Oooo! That one really scares me."

"We're going to start with Hot Potato. I need you all to get into a circle. This handy little plastic potato winds up and explodes when the timer expires. And I do mean explodes. Whoever's left holding it when it goes off is out of the game—really out of the game. Does everyone understand?" Spookie instructed. Something about the tone of his voice made me wonder about how safe this game would be.

The hot potato flew from one set of hands to another. The loud ticking it made was a little unnerving.

KABOOM! The potato shook, rattled, and blinked, but no pain followed the excruciatingly loud noise.

Our expressions changed from fear to relief. Hot Potato was only a game.

Within a few minutes most of the players had been eliminated. Only Frankie, Barry, Davis, Lisa, and I remained. Spookie looked us over, then said, "Let's make this game a little more interesting. I'm going to replace the plastic game potato with something that will give you a *real* bang."

Spookie reached into a deep pocket in his baggy clown pants. He pulled out a small black ball that looked like a cartoon-style bomb. "This is set for just a few seconds. Don't get stuck holding the bomb," the clown said with a sinister snicker.

I looked at Frankie and quietly asked, "Is Spookie trying to get rid of us because he thinks we're after the treasure? Maybe he heard us talking when we first came in. Remember? We thought he was just a stuffed head on the wall. I wonder if we said something to tip him off."

"Maybe. It must be worth a lot for him to go through all this trouble. Personally, I'd rather leave safely than find the treasure," she answered.

I responded, "I don't see how we can leave."

Then I had to focus on the bomb. Spookie had wound it and tossed it toward Lisa.

She gasped and pitched it into the air toward Davis.

Davis didn't even grab it. He batted it to Barry, who bobbled it. He yelled at me, "Find a window. Find someplace to get rid of this thing."

The little timer read thirteen seconds when Barry pitched it to Frankie. With her superb athletic ability, she had the bomb into the air and flying at me within seconds.

As I caught the sinister sphere, I yelled at Barry, "This can't be happening. A clown can't blow up a group of kids and expect to keep his business alive."

Spookie called out to me, "You better concentrate on keeping yourself alive."

I started to panic. I tried to pitch the bomb into a far corner where no kids were standing. But I took too long.

Time had run out. It was all over. I'd never see thirteen.

The red timer flashed zero. I turned my face away as I closed my eyes and waited for the explosion. Instead of a bang, I heard Spookie laugh. I opened my eyes in confusion.

When I looked at the bomb, the word *BANG!* flashed over and over again on the red light panel.

"Really funny," I said to Spookie.

"Oh, come on, birthday boy. Lighten up. We've only just begun. You're getting the best party package we offer, and there's a lot more frightening fun to come.

"Okay everyone, find a seat where you can see the velvet curtain. The magic show is about to begin," Spookie directed.

As we found places to sit, several clowns pulled the red velvet cloth aside to reveal a stage full of magic show props. I couldn't believe all that stood in front of us. Spookie the Clown had quite a setup.

In his first trick he put Penny the Party Crasher

into a box and sawed her in half. The special effects were great. I couldn't figure out how he did it until the trick was over and Penny broke out of the upper half of the box. Another clown jumped out of the lower half. Everybody cracked up.

"How embarrassing. It's so hard to find good help these days. Maybe if I used one of you for my next trick, it would turn out better." Spookie barely spoke the words before every kid in the room but me had a hand up in the air. Spookie laughed and pointed at a boy on the left of the room. He couldn't have chosen a more perfect candidate. The kid was always joking around, so being on stage would probably come naturally to him.

I watched as Spookie put the boy into a box and closed the door.

"I will say the magic words," Spookie said to his audience, "and right before your very eyes, one of your buddies will disappear."

Davis leaned over Frankie and whispered close to my ear. "I'm starting to get a bad feeling about this."

Spookie then said the magic words: "Treasure divine, treasure I'll find, treasure is mine."

What?! I thought. I could see the words had the same effect on the others who knew about the treasure.

"Spookie must be working with the ghosts to find the treasure," I whispered. "That's probably why he calls himself Spookie. We should have figured that out a long time ago."

I looked up at the stage. Spookie opened the box, but instead of our friend, a tall, sinister-looking clown with long, sharp fangs stepped out. Spookie tried to stop him, but the creepy clown pushed him away and started moving toward me and my friends.

Kids scattered everywhere. Frankie, Barry, and I made the mistake of running toward a corner of the room. The figure glided slowly in our direction.

"I think I believe the legend completely now," Frankie cried out.

"Lord, what should we do?" I prayed. I didn't realize I'd said it out loud until Frankie responded with a plan.

"Everybody run a different way," she said. "It might confuse him. Maybe we can all escape."

It wasn't a perfect plan, but then again this wasn't the perfect birthday party. I decided I'd be glad if I got home alive.

Barry shot to the right. Frankie shot to the left. I ran straight toward the tall clown's legs.

At the last possible second, I tried to dive between his large feet. I figured if I could get through his legs, I could be long gone before he could turn around. But he was quicker than I expected. He snatched me off the floor and held me high in the air. I found myself face to face with what I was now sure was one of the building's ghosts.

He growled loudly, "Now I've got you, and I guarantee that you won't get what you came for."

I closed my eyes and sent up a silent prayer for help.

I was afraid I'd soon join my friend who had disappeared.

I couldn't help myself; I peeked at the clown as he pulled me closer with one hand and raised his other hand in the air. I felt sure he was going to shove me into his mouth. Instead, the free hand reached for the top of his head and pulled off a mask.

"Happy Birthday, MacKenzie," the clown said. Without his mask, he didn't look the least bit creepy. He lowered me to the floor, and I dusted off my clothes.

"Thanks for the fright," I returned.

"Wow!" Spookie said as everyone started to calm down. "That was terrifying, wasn't it? If you'll all take your seats once again, we can continue with the magic show." Then he pulled the boy who had disappeared out of a hidden panel in the wall. The kid kept asking, "What happened? What happened?"

I went back to my seat, rather embarrassed that I had let the clown get the best of me. Frankie and Barry came up next to me.

"That was really brave when you tried to dive between his feet. It really drew his attention away from us. I was sure that we were all goners. This ghost thing has me on edge," Barry said.

"Me too," I agreed.

Davis joined us and said, "I was so worried that creep would eat you." He paused and added, "And then not floss."

I groaned and rolled my eyes.

Lisa said, "That was pretty scary, but I know it wasn't for real. If the ghost was just someone in a mask, maybe all the other stuff isn't real either . . ."

She sounded like she was trying to convince herself. I gave a small smile, and I hoped she was right.

After Spookie performed a few more magic tricks, he announced, "Now it's time to play hide-and-seek.

"In a moment, the doors behind the stage will open up, and you will have three minutes to run through. Find a place to hide before it comes after you," he instructed.

"Does he mean 'it' as in 'you're it' in a game? Or does he mean 'it' as in 'it lives in the basement and wants to protect its treasure'?" I asked.

Before anyone could answer me, the doors popped open, and everyone swarmed toward the stage.

When we ran through the door, we found ourselves in a big, dimly lit room. Huge Styrofoam shapes—squares, triangles, and columns—littered the floor. Kids ran to hide behind them. We also found tubes to crawl into and other shapes with holes cut in them. This game was going to be a blast!

Barry and I rolled out to our right and shot along the wall until we reached something that looked like a cave with an opening at each end.

"This will be perfect," Barry said. "If he sees us at one end, we can escape out the other."

I agreed and we crawled inside. I crept first as far into the shadows as I could. Then something grabbed me. I let out a small eek before I heard, "Hey, this is our spot." I recognized Frankie's voice immediately.

"What do you mean 'our spot'?" I asked.

"Lisa, Davis, and I got here first," she said. "But I guess there's enough room for everyone."

We fell silent when we heard a ghoulish cackle. "It" had just entered the room. We heard it grab one kid after another. Their screams echoed throughout the room. It was dragging away our friends one by one.

Soon everyone was caught but us. We could hear it move restlessly around the room as it searched for us. I held my breath and waited. I shifted silently, trying to find a more comfortable position.

I backed into someone and whispered, "I'm sorry." In the dark it was hard to tell who I'd bumped into.

I nearly yelled out when I received a hard shove to my ribs. I slammed forward into someone else.

"What are you doing?" Davis growled in a stern whisper.

"It wasn't my fault. Somebody pushed me from behind," I answered.

"That's impossible. We're all in front of you," Lisa said with a hint of panic in her voice.

"Then who pushed me?" I asked as fear seeped into my bones.

"I did," croaked a cold, dead voice behind us.

92

19

"Run! It's the ghost of Tremble Avenue!" I yelled to the others.

We flew out of the cave with Frankie leading the way. Screaming and sucking in air, we tried our best not to knock each other over in the confusion.

We stumbled around the room, hiding behind the various geometric shapes scattered around. I thought we were safe. Then I heard it shuffling across the floor behind me and to the right.

"Run!" I yelled to Lisa who had hidden with me. I decided right then that if I lived to see thirteen, I wouldn't have any more birthday parties, especially at Spookie the Clown's Halls of Pizza.

"Hey, ho, hey, kids! It's just me, Spookie the Clown. Come out, come out wherever you are. You five won the game! Everyone else has been caught and is waiting in the next room. Even it gave up and left," he told us.

"Then who was chasing us?" Davis asked.

"I don't know. There's only the six of us here," the clown answered.

I didn't believe him. I was sure Spookie's presence was keeping it from attacking us.

I started toward the door when I heard someone whisper, "Birthday boy, I'll be back with my gift later. Maybe I'll even stop by for some birthday cake and I scream."

"Let's get out of here, and I mean now," I commanded the others.

"That's right. It's time to go play musical chairs," Spookie cheerfully reported.

"No, I mean out of this Halls of Pizza place," I snapped at him.

"I'm sorry, but I can't let you do that. There is still so much more planned for this party, and we wouldn't want to disappoint any of our guests. So, let's all go back to the Hall of Games," Spookie said.

Since none of us knew the way out, we had to follow him.

When we entered the Hall of Games, I hoped to see the other guests waiting for us, but the room was empty. "Where is everyone?" I asked.

"It got them," the bizarre clown said without concern. I tried to press the question again, but Spookie put his hand over my mouth as he said, "Our last game will be musical chairs. Tonight we'll play a very special version. My helpers have set up five chairs.

You'll each have a place to sit when the music stops. But beware, one of the chairs . . . well, let's just say that you'll feel the earth move beneath your feet. Or rather beneath your seat."

"A trapdoor?" Frankie questioned in my direction. I shrugged my shoulders.

"We sometimes call this musical chairs that dance," Spookie reported. "Now, take your places. The music is about to begin."

Reluctantly, we walked around the circle of chairs when the music played. With each note our tension grew. We knew that one of us was headed for trouble, but which one?

When the music stopped, we tentatively chose chairs and sat. I looked around. My friends were all still there. Maybe the trapdoor system had broken. . . . In the next instant four chairs dropped through the floor, sending everyone but me to who knew where.

I gripped the sides of the seat. The chair rocked a little. I gasped and prepared to jump to safety when I looked up and saw that Spookie and his clown team had surrounded me.

Suddenly, the trapdoor seemed like the better of the two options. The clowns got to within a few feet of me before my chair went out from under me. I slipped down a cold, slick slide.

I zoomed past flashing lights that lined the slide.

I tried to focus on where I was heading. I shouldn't have.

Below my feet I saw a ball of flames licking toward the slide. I was heading straight toward it with no way to stop. I tried digging my heels into the slide, but it was too slick and I was going too fast.

Then I grabbed for the edges, but I couldn't feel anything to hold on to. I was only a yard or so away. I'd had a good twelve years. Too bad it would all come to an end in a few moments.

I closed my eyes and waited to feel the scorching heat of the flames. I slid for another few seconds, then I lost contact with the slide. I felt myself float through the air. I was too afraid to open my eyes.

I bounced to a landing on something soft. Then a bunch of hands grabbed and pulled at me.

"No, leave me alone. I don't want to die!" I screamed, squirming desperately to escape the tightening grips.

"Get a grip, Mac. What's your problem?" Frankie asked.

I opened my eyes and saw my four friends standing around me, trying to help me off the soft pillow I had landed on.

"What happened? Where are we? The last thing I saw was a ball of fire. Then I flew through the air without getting burned. Where are we?" I asked in bewilderment.

"We don't know. We just got here too," Lisa said.

She pointed at several orange strips of fabric fluttering around the pillow I had landed on. "These look a lot like flames when the air circulating system blows them around."

Frankie added, "That ball of fire thing looked pretty scary."

"Who was scared?" I asked, pretending that I hadn't been.

"You were," Barry blurted out.

I grimaced. "You're right. I was petrified," I said as Barry and Davis pulled me to my feet. "Spookie the Clown's Halls of Pizza is not at all what I expected. This place scares me to death. How did those kids from the party before us make it out of here without their hair standing on end?"

"They're braver than we are?" Lisa tossed out as a possibility.

Davis had been looking around the room and called back to us, "Hey, I don't know where we are, but I do know where we are heading. There is one door out of here, but it leads to the Hall of Fear. That sounds like a nice place to visit. I wonder if it's anywhere near the Tombs of Torture?"

"The Hall of Fear?" Lisa asked. "Do we really have to go there?"

"Remember what we studied in Sunday school last week, Lisa? I liked the verse so much I memorized it. Deuteronomy 31:8 says: 'The Lord himself . . . will be with you. He will not leave you or forget you. Don't be afraid. . . .' I think it's good to remember that God's always with us. Come on, let's try to find some other way out of here," Barry said.

To get the others moving, I told them, "I want to get out of here before Spookie and his clowns come for us."

Barry added, "Or worse, the ghosts."

Davis led the way, followed by Barry and Lisa. Frankie and I hurried along behind them. I said to her, "You're not as afraid as I am. Is there anything that really scares you?"

Frankie looked around as if she didn't want anyone else to hear her. "I do have this silly fear . . . you'll laugh if I tell," she said.

I shook my head to let her know I wouldn't laugh.

After a moment, she continued. "I'm afraid of the dark. I've always imagined that there is someone waiting for me at the top of our steps. Sometimes I'm afraid to go upstairs alone at night."

My mouth fell open. "I've always had that same fear," I blurted out. Then I quietly told Frankie how nice it was to be able to share my fears with her.

"Listen, if you two are finished whispering back there, could we get the show on the road?" Barry said to bring us back to our predicament. "Someone needs to enter the Hall of Fear and tell the others what it's like. I nominate the birthday boy since it's his party that got us into all this," Barry insisted.

Barry pulled the door open. All I could see was a pretty dark room. For some reason, I felt like we needed to be really quiet.

Frankie was standing right behind me. I could tell she felt the same way because she whispered, "I'll go in with you."

We started into the Hall of Fear. When nothing happened to us, the others followed cautiously behind us.

Lisa pointed at something and said in a stage whisper, "Over there. I see a tiny light blinking."

We went to investigate the light and found a booth that looked like *The Game of Life* in the Hall of Games.

"This is the only way out of here," Davis said.

Barry laughed and asked, "How do you know that?"

Davis pointed to a small sign on the door that said: This Is the Only Way Out.

Barry laughed again. "I guess you're right. Do we have any other choice?" Barry asked as he climbed into the booth.

Lisa stopped the rest of us from joining him. "I don't think we should all go in together. Let's split up so that at least some of us survive Spookie's to tell the world what really goes on here."

Barry butted in, "Great idea, but it won't work. Look at this control panel. The fuel gauge on this baby says empty, and by the looks of the controls, it must be preprogrammed. It may not come back to this room. We don't have any choice. We have to risk all of us going at once."

I inhaled deeply and let the air out slowly to try to relax. I wished again that Mom had never booked my party here. And I wished that I had never read chapter 13 in *Middletown's Ghosts and Ghouls*. Finally I prayed that we would all make it safely out of this place.

We crowded into the booth, and the door slid shut behind us. Even though we expected it to shut on us, the sound of it closing made us jump.

We watched the red numbers on the control panel count down from ten to nine to eight . . . all the way to zero. Then we felt the booth start to shake and rumble.

On the viewing screen before us we could see that we were climbing slowly. We passed through an opening in the roof and continued to climb into the air. The buildings, cars, and people below us looked smaller and smaller. Without warning, the booth stopped high in the air.

"What happened?" I asked. I was so frightened by the height that I felt dizzy.

"I think we're stuck at the top of a long pole,"

a high, shrill voice said. It took me a few seconds to figure out that Davis had spoken. *He must be really scared,* I thought.

"Why do you think that?" I asked.

Davis pointed across the skyline. When he answered me, he talked way too fast. "Look over there. There's another booth on a pole. That pole doesn't look strong enough to hold a bird up."

"Now what?" Barry cried.

"I don't think we have many options. I guess we have to wait and see what happens," I told the others.

"Why is this booth just sitting up here?" Lisa asked as she choked back tears.

"Heights scare some people pretty badly," Frankie told her. She tried to keep her voice as calm as possible to soothe Lisa.

"But we're just sitting here and not doing anything. I want down before this thing starts to rock back and forth. Ahhh! I should never have opened my mouth. We're starting to rock," Lisa yelled.

"Calm down. A little wobble would be normal at this height," Barry said, trying to reassure her. But the whole booth tipped so far to one side that we all screamed while we slid around on the seat.

I just knew the booth was going to break off the pole. We were goners for sure.

We held each other tight, but it didn't stop the fear from getting a good hold on us too. I wanted out. Now!

"We've got to get out of here," I yelled. Beads of perspiration formed on my forehead.

"How?" Davis screamed back. Terror poured out along with his question.

Barry scrambled toward a red flashing button on the control panel.

"Barry, what are you trying to do?" I yelled.

"This might be the way down. We've got to try it." He almost reached the button, but then the booth dipped backward. We all slid toward the back wall. When the contraption tipped forward again, Barry practically fell on top of the button.

As soon as he touched the flashing red spot, we felt the booth straighten up. Then we started to descend. We cheered, but our joy didn't last long. We had started to fall so quickly that our landing could flatten us permanently.

"This can't get any worse," Frankie moaned.

"Oh yes, it can," Lisa responded as her eyes widened in panic.

She started shaking like a flag in the wind as she shrieked, "We're breaking up. Look! Cracks!"

I looked down where Lisa pointed and saw a bunch of small cracks. Then I looked at the walls. Like lightning bolts flashing through the sky, jagged cracks split the wall panels.

I knew we'd never make it to the ground before the booth split into a zillion pieces.

"Hang on to something!" Davis bellowed.

As the booth around us broke apart, we braced ourselves for the long fall to earth.

I hit the ground much sooner than I expected. Nothing hurt. How could that be? Was I dead? I quickly ran my hands along my arms and legs to see if I were intact. Then I reached for my head. Still there. I finally felt brave enough to open my eyes.

I couldn't believe it. I sat up and in the dim light I saw that my friends were right beside me, all in perfect shape. The whole time the booth had only been a few feet off the ground. The terrifying experience had all just been special effects.

"What was that all about?" Barry asked, shaking his head.

"Fear," answered Frankie simply. "We were in the Hall of Fear. We faced the fear of heights, the fear of falling, and the fear of death. What's left?"

Davis spotted a door that we'd missed earlier. As he walked toward it, he said, "I don't care what happens next as long as it gets us out of here."

We pulled ourselves together and scrambled to follow him. The door led to another dark room. We could hear the wind whistling and bat wings flapping all around us.

"Where are we?" I asked.

No one answered. We had all heard the sound of heavy footsteps and deep breathing. It had to be one of the ghosts. The sound got closer and closer.

An excruciating screech cut through the darkness.

"Run!" somebody yelled. But it wasn't necessary. Our shoe soles were already slapping the hard floor.

We ran through another door and ended up in a long hallway. None of us knew where it led, but we could see another door at its end.

Frankie was right in front of me. I could hear her say over and over to herself: "Run, Frankie, run."

My birthday party seemed more like a nightmare every minute. I wished Spookie's had turned out to be safe and boring. Maybe a little pizza and a little birthday cake and pin the tail on the donkey would have been fun.

I watched as Davis, Barry, and Lisa shot through the door at the end of the hall. Then I realized the sounds behind us had stopped.

"Frankie, wait up. I don't hear anything behind us anymore."

She stopped at the doorway and looked into the room.

"MacKenzie, I don't want to go in there. It's so dark. I hate the dark," she said. I could tell she was really afraid.

I wanted to tell her I was afraid too when a blood-curdling scream crackled through the darkness.

"What do we do?" Frankie asked.

"We've got to go help whoever that was. Maybe we can find a light switch," I answered.

We slipped through the door and slid along the wall using our hands as our eyes. I was also praying that we would discover the way out.

Something tapped me on my shoulder. I turned my head to see what Frankie wanted.

But it wasn't her voice I heard.

"Birthday boy, do you still have the treasure?"

I gulped as hands gripped my shoulders and squeezed them tight. *What treasure did he think I had?*

It had to be one of the ghosts! I shook off the hands and spun around to face him. In the dim light from the doorway I watched as he grabbed Frankie.

My blood ran cold. I panicked.

"Let her go!" I demanded as I lunged forward. The only thing in my mind was that I had to save my friend. But I misjudged the distance and missed.

The ghost dragged her, kicking and screaming, deeper into the room.

"Wait," I yelled. "I'm the birthday boy. Take me, not her."

His sinister laugh cut into me.

"Come and take her away from me," he taunted.

In the next second the darkness engulfed them. I ran to where they had been standing.

"I don't think this is part of the birthday party games." The voice startled me, and I nearly had a cardiac arrest.

"Barry, is that you?" I blurted out. Then I asked,

"Where are the others?"

"Right here. We saw that ghoul drag Frankie over here," Davis answered.

"We've got to find her," Lisa pleaded.

"We will. Frankie's screams ended too abruptly. There has to be a door on this wall. Help me find it," I urged.

I ran my hands along the wall. When they hit a button, I pushed it. The wall spun around, taking me with it.

Suddenly, a door across the room opened, admitting a little light. I still couldn't see the ghost, but I heard him calling to me: "Birthday boy."

My eyes started to adjust to the dim light. I walked toward the open door and read the sign over it: Hall of Amazing Mazes. I couldn't believe it. How would I find my way through a maze in near darkness? I stepped into the room. I could either go to the right or the left.

"The Lord himself . . . will be with you. He will not leave you or forget you. Don't be afraid. . . ." I heard myself repeating the Bible verse out loud.

I began to feel calmer, secure that I wasn't alone.

"Help, Ralph!" I heard Frankie yell. *Ralph? Who was Ralph?* Then I got it. She must be able to see me, even though I couldn't see her. Ralph was an expression we used to call out directions. If you wanted someone to turn right, you said, "Hang a Ralph." Frankie was directing me through the maze.

I turned to my right. When I came to another choice, I needed help again.

I yelled, "Louie, are you out there?" Louie was the code word for left. I heard a muffled noise in response, so I turned left.

I didn't get very far before I had to make another choice. "Louie?" I yelled. No answer.

Then I called out, "It's Ralph." Still no answer. The ghost must have figured out our code. I went to the right and came to a dead end. I turned and ran back the other way.

When I had to make another decision, I heard Frankie yell, "Ralph, Help me."

I was getting closer. Her voice sounded near.

As I stumbled into another hallway, I saw a dark staircase. Behind me a door slammed shut with a resounding bang. I turned around and discovered that the door had locked.

My only option was the stairs. At the top, I saw the ghastly grayish figure. Frankie stood right next to him.

"Birthday boy," the ghost called in his raspy, gasping voice. "I've been waiting for you. I'm willing to exchange your friend for the treasure. Come on, birthday boy."

"But I don't have any treasure. Please let her go," I pleaded.

He only cackled and held Frankie in front of him so I could see her. "Here she is. Are you willing to trade?"

"Let her go!" I screamed, trying to make myself sound menacing.

The ghost taunted me with his laughter. I felt terrible. I was too afraid to go up the steps to save my friend. All my life, I'd had that terrible fear that something was waiting for me at the top of a dark stairway. I never thought I'd have to face it.

Although the fear was almost overwhelming, I had to help Frankie.

I took the first step. My legs went weak. My knees

seemed to turn into jelly, but I forced myself to keep climbing.

"Birthday boy, it's time for you to give me back my treasure. Have you brought it?" the ghost asked again.

I closed my eyes, lowered my head, and charged up the remaining steps. I planned to ram myself into the ghost. Then again, if it was a ghost, maybe I would pass right through it. The thought startled me, and I opened my eyes.

The ghost had disappeared. I saw Frankie standing there alone.

"Frankie, where did the ghost go?" I asked frantically.

"He went through that door, MacKenzie," Frankie told me. "I'm so glad he's gone. I was afraid I'd never get free. Let's go back through the maze and get out of here."

I thought for a moment. "We can't," I told her slowly. "A door locked behind me. I guess the only way out of here is to follow the ghost of Tremble Avenue."

Frankie looked pretty unhappy about that idea. "Where are the others?" she asked, stalling for time.

"I don't know. They didn't come with me through the maze. I hope we can find them when we get out of here," I responded.

Frankie seemed to have made up her mind to be

brave. "Let's go, MacKenzie. The longer I wait, the harder it's going to be to walk through this door."

I gave her a smile. "Here goes nothing," I said. I pushed on the door, and it popped open.

"Careful. The ghost may be waiting for you on the other side," she reminded me.

I eased the door open and looked cautiously through the opening.

"Ho, hey, ho!" Spookie boomed at us. "We thought we'd lost you. It's time to open your present."

"Where is everyone?" I demanded.

"Right this way. They're waiting to watch you open your gift. It's from everyone here at Spookie the Clown's Halls of Pizza. We want you to know how much we've appreciated being able to give you this very special party. It isn't every day that a group of your fame celebrates a birthday here," he said.

What he said confused me. What kind of special group were we?

He led us back to the Hall of Food, where some of my friends had gathered. I still didn't see Barry, Lisa, and Davis, or the kids that disappeared in *The Game of Chance.* One of Spookie's clowns shoved a large box into my hands.

"What's this?" I asked.

"That's the gift I was telling you about. Come on in here and sit down," Spookie said.

I sat down in the seat with the big box on my lap.

"Go ahead and open it," Spookie encouraged.

I was afraid to. It could have been a box of snakes, exploding bombs, insects, or anything. I just stared at it.

"Hey, are you going to open it?" Frankie asked.

"Would you?" I responded.

"No, but then again, I'm not the birthday boy, am I?" she said.

Spookie looked at me kind of funny, as if he couldn't believe a twelve-year-old wouldn't want to tear into a present. Then he shrugged his shoulders and said, "Okay, if you aren't going to open the gift, we'll have some cake and ice cream. Bring in the food," he yelled.

Several clowns rolled two big carts into the room. One had a cake on it in the shape of Spookie's head. The other cart held a gigantic tub of vanilla ice cream.

Spookie led the kids in the room through a loud and off-key rendition of "Happy Birthday to You."

Then he said, "Okay, birthday boy, you cut the cake, then you get to dish out the ice cream. That's a tradition here at Spookie's."

"You've only been open a week. How could you have traditions already?" Frankie asked.

"We are very old in our hearts. Now the cake," he insisted.

I half expected something to jump out when I sank the knife into the thick white icing and chocolate cake. I sliced a number of pieces then handed Frankie the knife to cut more.

"Now for the ice cream," Spookie said as he slapped the ice-cream scoop into my hand. "Dig in, but I want to warn you that the ice cream is very hard, so use a little muscle."

I thought to myself that Spookie was a very strange clown. I've scooped ice cream before. I didn't need that much instruction.

I stepped over to the cart holding the ice cream. The container was huge. It certainly looked like more than enough to go around.

I looked at Spookie and said, "You and your clowns are welcome to share in my birthday cake and ice cream. Of course, around here, maybe we should call it birthday cake and I scream."

"No, thanks," he said through his clown makeup smile. "Just go ahead and serve the kids."

I leaned over the ice cream and asked Frankie, "How much do you want?"

"Mmmm. I really like ice cream. Can I have two or three scoops?" she requested.

"Sure," I said as I began to dip the scoop into the frozen dessert. I remembered what Spookie had said and pressed down hard. To my surprise, the scoop sank into the ice cream as if it were a melting milk-

119

shake. Before I could stop my motion, I was dipped up to my elbow in the white foam.

Another one of Spookie's stupid jokes, I thought as I pulled my hand out of the ooze. Something tugged on my arm from deep inside the ice cream. I pulled back. Then I saw the hand with long, sharp nails reaching out of the ice cream. The ghost!

I pulled hard in an attempt to free my arm, but the ghoul dragged me deeper into the vat. I felt the gooey ooze at my ear.

The next thing I knew, two hands had grabbed my shoulders and saved me from the fake ice cream. The ghost's hand slipped off my arm, and I popped out of the ooze. I stumbled backward, staring at the ice-cream tub.

Spookie made a huge show of wiping me off and apologizing as his helpers wheeled the cart of ice cream out of the room. "I'm sorry," he said. "Our ice cream always comes frozen solid. Someone must have left it out to make it easier to scoop. Apparently it got left out too long. I'm so sorry about the mess."

"Didn't you see the hand that grabbed me and tried to pull me in?" I asked frantically.

"Maybe you encountered a wild vanilla bean, but I don't think they're strong or vicious enough to pull you in. Your strong scooping motion must have made you lose your balance. You fell in," he explained. "Besides, those tubs of ice cream aren't deep enough for something to have hidden inside it."

"But I know something pulled on my arm. It was probably the same thing that took Frankie through the Amazing Maze."

"Amazing Maze? . . . If it will make you feel better, I'll have BooBoo the Clown bring the ice cream back so you can see there's nothing in it."

BooBoo answered, "Sorry, Spookie, but we already poured that stuff into the garbage can out back. Here's another tub so the kids can have their party treat."

"I guess I can't prove anything to you, but we can get this wild and crazy party going again. BooBoo, you dish up the rest of the cake and ice cream. While he does that, MacKenzie, why don't you go ahead and open your gift?" Spookie was all smiles.

"So many weird things have happened here, I'm not sure that I want to open this gift," I answered.

"Go ahead. Open it. I picked it out especially for you. Here, I'll help." Spookie grabbed the gift from my lap and started ripping the paper off.

I grabbed it back.

"Okay, I'll open it. After all, it is my gift," I said. I pulled the bow off and tossed it to the floor.

I ripped the remaining paper off the box. Then I pulled the top off, revealing a Spookie the Clown plastic snow globe.

A roar of noise surrounded me.

I jumped, almost dropping the snow globe. In the same motion, I turned around to see where all the noise had come from. The rest of my party guests had entered from another room. I saw all the kids I thought were missing.

"MacKenzie, this is the greatest party I've ever been to," several of them said in unison.

Barry and Davis ran up to me.

"Mac, watch out. It all looks like everyone's having fun, but don't forget the ghost," Davis whispered.

The other kids lined up to get cake and ice cream from BooBoo. I could tell from all the noise that they were having a great time. Barry plopped down next to me.

"What happened to you guys? I thought we planned to stay together. I had to make my way through a maze alone in the dark." I felt annoyed with my friends, even though I was relieved to see they were safe.

He smiled at me and said, "We tried to follow you, but we couldn't figure out how you got that wall to flip around. Then Spookie showed up out of nowhere and led us back to the Hall of Games. He said that you'd meet us there. We didn't see you, but other groups kept joining us. Then Spookie's clowns brought us in here. Thanks for starting the cake and ice cream without us," he teased.

Lisa came over and joined us. "It sure looks like everyone's having a blast," she said. "Most of the kids keep saying they want to throw their next party here. I think you've started a real fad."

Davis said, "But none of them saw the ghost, and none of them went through the Hall of Fear. To them it's just the most fantastic birthday celebration they've ever been to."

Barry added, "You're going to be a legend. The whole school is going to know about the kind of parties that you throw."

"Personally, I just want out of here. Before you came in, the ghost tried to pull me into a tub of melted ice cream," I whispered.

Spookie called for our attention. When everyone had quieted down, he announced, "I hate to say this, but our party is almost over. If you enjoyed yourself, tell everyone. If you didn't like the place, don't tell anyone." Then he broke into his goofy laugh. "Ho, hey, ho!"

"I don't hate to say this party is over," Frankie whispered to the rest of us. "Spookie acts as if he doesn't even know what's going on. He seems oblivious to the ghost roaming around in his Halls of Pizza."

Spookie said, "But before you all head home, I want to do one last magic trick. I need a volunteer. Well, not actually a volunteer—someone has made a special request for MacKenzie Griffin to be a part of this trick."

"What do I do?" I asked the other four.

"Maybe Spookie doesn't know about the ghost. If not, he can't be in on it. All his other tricks seemed pretty safe. Go ahead and finish out the party with one last blast," Barry advised quickly and quietly.

"If the ghost gets me, you won't be my best friend anymore," I warned Barry.

He responded with a smile, "If the ghost gets you, can I have your new bike?"

I didn't have a chance to answer. Spookie's clowns surrounded me and lifted my chair high into the air. They carried me across the room and set me on the stage next to Spookie.

He waved his hand in my direction and said, "This is a very simple trick. I will lay this piece of cloth over MacKenzie."

He dropped a thick, black piece of material over me. As it hit my head, I felt a platform start to lower, and Spookie's voice trailed off. I looked up, and a wire shaped like the back of the chair gave the illusion that I was still sitting on stage.

The platform lowered into a dingy little room below the floor. I could see a tall, dark shape in the poorly lit corner.

I had a bad feeling. I knew I had seen this silhouette before.

He took a large step closer and asked in a menacing growl, "Have you come to return my treasure?"

"I don't have your treasure. We never found any treasure," I stammered at the ghost. "I don't know why you think we have it. Please just let me go home."

"I can't let that happen," he answered me.

"Any second now, Spookie is going to bring this platform back to the floor, and I better be in the chair or . . . or . . . or . . ."

"Or what?" the ghost asked in an icy voice. "I control the platform with this button." The ghost pointed a long, sharp nail at the button. "Where is my treasure?"

"What treasure? I don't have any treasure," I pleaded.

I felt my eyes fill with tears. But I couldn't cry. I couldn't let him know how frightened I was.

The ghoul stared deep into my eyes. He opened his mouth and sneered out, "Give me back my treasure. Penny the Party Crasher stole it from me and gave it to you."

I sagged in relief. The tokens! All he wanted was the tokens Penny had "pulled" out of my ear. The other kids had taken lots of them, but I had some somewhere. I dug into my left pocket. None there. I must have put them in my right pocket. Hmm, not there either. I thrust my hands deeply into every pocket in my clothing. Nothing.

The ghost took another step closer.

I frantically braced myself in the chair. My hand brushed the plastic snow globe Spookie had given me. Maybe the ghost would take that and leave me alone.

He didn't want the cheap globe. I eyed the button that would take me back up to Spookie.

"Don't think that you're going to get away until I have what I want," my captor said in his raspy voice.

Think, MacKenzie! You've got to get out of here, I said to myself. If only I could find a way to push the button.

I stretched my arm out, but I couldn't reach far enough.

"Naughty birthday boy, are you trying to leave so soon? And just when I was enjoying myself," the gray, grim form teased.

As much as I hated soccer drills, even that sounded better than being at the mercy of this ghoul.

Soccer! That was it! That was my answer.

My aim was pretty good. I bet I could kick

Spookie's snow globe across the little room and strike the button with it.

The ghost moved around to my left side, and I pretended to make a move to my right. I faked him out, and I had a clear shot at the button.

I kicked. Thwump!

The globe sailed through the air. The ghost realized what I had done and dived through the air to stop the flying globe.

I held my breath, and I closed my eyes. I didn't want to see what would happen. It was my only chance to escape. If the ghost stopped the globe, I was doomed.

Then I heard the plastic ball crash. Did it hit the button? Did it hit the wall? Did the ghost knock it to the ground?

All I could do was pray.

I felt the platform and chair jerk. I started to rise!

I looked over and saw the ghost lying on the floor. He tried to get up, but the plastic orb had smashed, splashing its liquid all over the floor. He slipped on it and fell back to the ground.

Ascending into the black cloth, I could hear Spookie say, "I think our birthday boy has finally returned from the great beyond. I've never had anyone take so long to come back before. I do hope . . ."

I startled Spookie the Clown by ripping off the black cloth and running for the exit.

"Where are you going, MacKenzie?" Spookie called after me.

"My mother should be here by now. She hates it when I'm late. In fact, she grounds me. I've got to go," I yelled over my shoulder as I ran out.

When I got to the door, I stopped and motioned for everyone to follow. The entire group of party guests raced out behind me.

I heard a familiar voice say, "So, how was the party, Kiddo?"

Only one person ever called me Kiddo. It was my mom. The only thing that I wanted to do was to get out of Spookie's.

I didn't have to tell my mother anything about the party. All the other kids were telling their parents about the fantastic time they'd had. Most of them asked to have their next party at Spookie's.

I smiled and nodded my head. My party was a hit. I might have been scared to death by the ghosts haunting the building, but everyone else had a great time.

"Give me a moment to pay and thank Spookie for the great time you all had, then we can get going," my mom said.

Frankie and Lisa walked up behind me. Lisa asked, "Did you have another run-in with the ghost while you were under that cloth?"

"Yes, I thought I was a goner for sure."

"So did we," Barry said as Davis put his hand on my shoulder.

"I can't believe we're getting out of here safe. I'm going to hurry Mom up so we all can go home," I told them as I walked to the counter where Mom was paying for the party.

Spookie had handed her a business card, and she slid it to me to carry home. As my mom wrote a check, I leaned over and read the desk calendar by the phone. I wondered what other groups would have to face the ghosts of Spookie's Halls of Pizza.

Suddenly, my mouth dropped open and my head became light. I couldn't believe what I read. Written over today's date was "National Horror Movie Fan Club Birthday Party." Underneath was a memo that said, "Rent ghost costumes and really scare the kids." Across Saturday's date I saw my name.

Spookie had written the wrong party groups on the wrong days. I had gotten the party for the Horror Movie Fan Club.

The greatest birthday party of my life was all a mistake. Cool!

I smiled at her and said, "Mom, we're ready to go."

"Good, wait for me in the minivan. I'll only be a few seconds," she responded in her usual joyful way.

As I walked up to the others, I looked down at Spookie's business card. Below the words *Spookie the Clown's Halls of Pizza* was imprinted *Alexander S. Pookie, Owner and Chief Executive Clown.* I chuckled to myself. The name Spookie had nothing to do with ghosts. It was actually the clown's name, S. Pookie.

I told the others, "Mom said for us to wait for her in the van."

We all started to head outside. Before I left, I wanted to look around at the greatest party place in the world. Just then something floated down on my head.

Looking up at the stuffed heads on the walls, I gasped.

For a second I had seen one of the gray clown ghosts, and it winked at me. I blinked and it disappeared.

I shook my head and noticed another flower petal float to the ground.

I knew it was only someone in a costume. I whistled and strolled out the door to the sidewalk. As the door swung shut behind me, I was sure I heard someone say in a raspy voice, "Good-bye, birthday boy."

I ran to the van.

Stay Away From The Swamp

Book #8
by Fred E. Katz

I let go of the vine and landed inside the jail tree's ring of vines. Say, this made a pretty good hiding place. If the swamp weren't so spooky, I wouldn't mind a hideaway like this.

"Man," Hammer puffed. He moved slowly toward me. "I thought you were done for. I thought one of the ghost snakes had taken control of the vine."

Hammer shuffled closer. He held out a hand. "Hey, Clint? You okay? You didn't break any bones, did you?"

"Nah," I croaked. I clasped Hammer's hand and hauled myself to my feet. Then I looked at my hands. They were covered with green plant stains. It had been nothing but a vine after all.

I went back to the vine and gave it a push. It swayed gently. I forced strength into my voice. "A vine."

"What?" Hammer didn't catch what I'd said.

"Never mind. Check this place out, Hammer. It's kind of cool. You can almost hide in here."

Hammer looked around the dark enclosure.

"I see what you mean. But I don't think it's cool. I think it's creepy. Come on, let's get to the cabin and get this over with."

"Hold it, Hammer! Look!"

"Yikes!" said Hammer when he saw my discovery. The soft, mossy mound was only camouflage. We had found the door to the ghost snakes' tunnel.

"Come on, let's go," I said, putting my hand to the entrance to the tunnel.

"What? Are you out of your mind? You can't go in there! And you certainly can't open the door. Do you want them to know we've discovered their passageway?"

What Hammer said made sense. I wasn't convinced we were dealing with ghosts, but we still could've caused some serious trouble by disturbing the tunnel. Whoever or whatever used this tunnel didn't need to know we'd found it.

"Where do you suppose it leads?" I wondered.

"My theory is that it leads all over town. Of course, it depends how far the ghosts have gone in their conquests."

Maybe you're right, Hammer. But since when do ghosts need tunnels to move around? They can be invisible if they want," I observed.

"That may be true," Hammer said, "but ghosts may need a place where they can drag their . . . victims."

We both shuddered. Suddenly the hideaway didn't seem so cozy after all.

"Come on, we've found what you were looking for, haven't we? Let's go," Hammer said.

"Not yet. This just raises more questions. The cabin is only a short way from here. Let's go," I answered.

We walked through more clumps of weeds and grass.

"Cut around to the right," I said.

I hadn't meant to speak so softly . . . as if I were afraid something would hear me.

We crept around the jail tree. I thought we'd never get to the other side. Was the jail tree spreading too? Just like the whole swamp seemed to be?

At last we made it to the top of the little hill and peered down at the cabin.

The roof looked much steeper than I remembered. It seemed to point toward the sky. It made the cabin look like a ghostly rocket.

"Three Bears' house, huh?" Hammer's voice made me jump. "They must have painted it with coal tar."

"Let's go." I started down the hill before I could lose my nerve. Hammer stayed at my side.

"Here's the first window I looked in," I told my friend. "Kristin claims she saw three bears sitting on chairs in here."

"What?" Hammer said. "You're kidding, right?"

We cupped our hands around our eyes and pressed our faces to the window. As before, I felt dust creep up my nose and settle in my throat. I stepped back from the window and sneezed.

That same instant Hammer let out a scream.